"You've traveled far?" she asked.

He laughed shortly. "Farther than you know."

‹‹‹ ›››

*S*he stared at her pale fingers wrapped in his. *We must have come from the same place,* she thought with growing excitement. "Are you my brother?"

"No, I'm not. We are not related."

"Good," she answered before she could stop herself. She felt a blush rising to her cheeks and was grateful that he couldn't see it.

He was rubbing the back of her hand with his thumb, and her skin tingled where his touched hers. *James did the same thing to my hand two days ago and it felt good, exciting, but nothing like this. . . . Something about him feels so right, even though I don't know him.*

She was suddenly nervous; the silence around them felt like the air did when a storm approached from across the sea. She spoke just to calm herself. "You've been searching how long?"

"Thirteen years."

"How did you know it was me if you haven't seen me in so long?"

"How does the whale know when to swim to warmer waters for winter? How do the fish know when a predator is near? How do you know when love is real? You just know."

"Once Upon a Time . . ." is timely again with these new tales:

THE STORYTELLER'S DAUGHTER
by Cameron Dokey

BEAUTY SLEEP
by Cameron Dokey

SNOW
by Tracy Lynn

MIDNIGHT PEARLS
by Debbie Viguié

From Simon Pulse
Published by Simon & Schuster

MIDNIGHT
PEARLS

Debbie Viguié

SIMON PULSE
New York   London   Toronto   Sydney   Singapore

This book is a work of fiction. Any references to historical events, real
people, or real locales are used fictitiously. Other names, characters, places, and
incidents are the product of the author's imagination, and any resemblance to
actual events or locales or persons, living or dead, is entirely coincidental.

First Simon Pulse edition June 2003

Copyright © 2003 by Debbie Viguié

SIMON PULSE
An imprint of Simon & Schuster
Children's Publishing Division
1230 Avenue of the Americas
New York, NY 10020

Designed by Debra Sfetsios
The text of this book was set in Adobe Jenson.

Printed in the United States of America
2 4 6 8 10 9 7 5 3 1

Library of Congress Control Number 2002115624

ISBN 0-689-85557-5

✠✠✠✠✠✠

To Nancy Holder, for believing in me

I would like to thank Lisa Clancy, the world's greatest editor,
and Lisa Gribbin, who keeps things running smoothly. Thank
you to my husband, Scott, who stayed up late with me countless
nights so I could discuss the story with him. Thank you to my
father, Rick Reynolds, the greatest brainstorming partner
anyone could ever ask for. Thank you to my mother, Barbara
Reynolds, without whose love and support this would not be
possible. Thank you to Mrs. Voget and Miss Romer,
who always challenged me to do my best.

✠✠✠✠✠✠

❖ Prologue ❖

It should have been the happiest day of her life, but instead it was a living nightmare. Pearl slowly fingered the fabric of her pale blue gown and closed her eyes. Fat tears squeezed out from beneath her eyelids and rolled down her cheeks.

The bell of the chapel began to ring. It was ringing for her. Its keening was her death sentence, its steady beat her death march. She felt herself begin to shake. Today was the last day of her freedom, her last taste of joy. She opened her eyes and stared down at her slippers. They gleamed softly white, mocking her. Today was supposed to be the happiest day of her life, for today she would become a bride.

She looked back upon her life and saw how every step had led her here. Where had it all gone wrong? What could she have changed?

She closed her eyes again and prayed for death.

❖ Chapter One ❖

The fisherman sat quietly in his boat staring at the darkening skies. The sun should have stood directly overhead, marking midday, but instead it was obscured by angry clouds that seemed to grow thicker by the moment. He squinted, staring at the horizon. The leathery skin of his face crinkled around his hazel eyes. A storm was coming up fast, too fast. A stiff wind suddenly sprang to life, roaring across the bow of the boat and bringing with it the unmistakable smell of rain. It was time to head for shore.

The fish had been acting strange all day, nervous, as though there was a predator lurking in the darkening water. He had been out since noon, and not a single one had found its way into his nets. Still, he had seen the dancing shadows and quick flashes of silver that indicated their presence. He quickly pulled the woven rope nets in and secured them.

A raindrop splatted on his nose and a shiver danced up his spine. *Finneas*, he thought, *you'd better get yourself home fast.*

No sooner had he picked up the oars and began to row than the heavens let loose. The ocean began to heave, and it was all he could do to keep the tiny boat from capsizing.

He strained at the oars with all his might. He had never seen a storm come up so quickly. He should have had time to make it home before the weather became this bad. His arms began to ache with the strain of fighting the waves. A huge one bore down on him, and he saw it through the rain, but it was too late to turn the boat. It crested over the bow and filled the tiny vessel with water.

He had always been careful, always respected the sea not only for what it could give but also for what it could take. He had lost his father and his two brothers to its wrath. His was a family of fishermen eking out a living from the sea. But the sea was a fickle mistress. He remembered the storm that had taken the lives of the other men in his family. Still, he, too, had gone to the sea for his livelihood. It was all he knew.

As wave after wave continued to crash down upon him, he knew that his time had come at last. The sea would claim him this day, and he would never see his beloved Mary again. He whispered a desperate prayer to St. Michael, patron saint of the sea, and another one to King Neptune for good measure. Father Gregory would not be happy about that, but the good father wasn't there to take offense.

A short distance ahead of him he saw a light shimmering in the water that grew brighter as he watched. Was it the angel of death coming to take him? He briefly thought about trying to go around the spot. He was too tired, though, to waste his strength rowing the extra distance. *And if it is the angel of death,* he reasoned, *he'll find me whether I turn the boat or not.* He kept his course, and moments later he was right above the light. He stared down into the water but could see nothing.

Cast out your nets, a voice whispered in his head. Without thinking, Finneas scurried to comply, heaving the nets over the side and dropping them down into the light. Something heavy caught in them, and he feared that between the weight and the raging of the ocean the ropes would snap. He began to pull them in. They held, and the light grew brighter as he kept pulling. At last something broke the surface of the water.

Finneas gasped as the small face of a child looked up at him. She had enormous eyes that shone dark against her pale skin. Her white hair floated on the water, each long strand glimmering with a greenish light—the glow that he had seen. She was caught in his net, and he heaved her into the boat. She sat very still, the blinking of her eyes the only sign of life.

He quickly untangled her until she sat naked and shivering in the bottom of the tiny vessel. He peeled off his coat and wrapped it around her. For a moment he forgot the wind and waves and storm as he stared at her. *What had Father Gregory read from the Good Book that morning?* "I will make you fishers of men."

He smiled reassuringly at the child as he picked up his oars. "We are going to make it, you and I." She just blinked her enormous eyes.

God, Neptune, St. Michael—someone had sent the child to him. He couldn't let her die in the storm. That conviction gave him the will to keep pulling at the oars. At last after what seemed like an eternity, the wind swept aside a curtain of rain and he caught a glimpse of the shore. His heart lifted at the sight, and he pulled on the oars with renewed strength.

Finally they hit the beach. He scrambled out of the boat and began to try to pull it backward onto the sand. Finneas fell to his knees, a sob escaping him. He was too weak. He felt his fingers beginning to slip from the bow when, suddenly, strong hands closed over his and lent their strength. Together they pulled the ship backward up onto the beach.

Finneas collapsed onto the sand gasping and looked up to see his wife. His heart filled at the sight of her face, beautiful in his eyes. "Mary, I thought I'd never see you again."

"And I you," she answered.

He gestured to the boat. "I brought you something."

She looked in and gasped softly. "Oh my."

They made it to the house and barred the door against the lashing rain. Finneas peeled off his wet clothes, depositing them in a heap by the fire and changing into dry ones while Mary wrapped the child in a warm blanket. She sat down with her by the fire and lifted a lock of her wet hair. Finneas noticed that the glow from the child's hair was slowly fading.

He shivered and muttered a silent prayer. Still, as he looked into the little girl's enormous eyes, he couldn't see any evil lurking in them. *If she isn't of the devil, then she has to be from God.* He nodded slowly. She was God's gift to his Mary, who had no child of her own. He placed a hand on Mary's shoulder.

When Mary looked up at him he had no answers for the questions in her eyes. They stared at each other for several minutes before she broke the silence.

"I thought you might be dead," she croaked, her voice hoarse.

"I nearly was," he admitted as he took a seat beside her. "Then I found her—out there in the water. I knew then that I was going to live and that the Good Lord wanted me to bring her home—to you."

Mary gently stroked the girl's hair. "She can't be more than four years old. What do you think she was doing out there by herself?"

Finneas shook his head. "I don't know."

The girl stirred in Mary's arms and stretched her small hand out toward the fire. Her skin was pale, deathly pale. Finneas felt his heart begin to pound. For a moment, when her hand was up in front of the fire, he imagined that he'd been able to see right through the skin, through her very hand, to see the fire glowing on the other side.

He shook his head to clear it. *I'm exhausted, and a*

trick of the light sent my imagination on a flight of fancy. That is all. But beside him he heard Mary gasp, and when she turned to him with fearful eyes he knew that it was no trick and that she had seen it too.

"Wh-what is she?"

He met Mary's eyes. "I don't know and I don't think we want to know."

She nodded slowly, and a silent agreement stretched between them. The child looked up at them questioningly. She stretched out her other hand from beneath the blanket. It was balled into a tight fist. Something dark shone through the cracks between her fingers.

"What have you got, little one?" Finneas asked, reaching gently to take her hand. He pushed at her fingers, and reluctantly her fist began to open.

There in her palm was the largest pearl he had ever seen. It was a shiny, midnight blue color and was almost perfectly round. He had never seen anything like it.

Her small fingers balled around it, and her hand disappeared back beneath the blanket. He laid a hand upon her head. "I think we'll call her Pearl."

Two days later the storm had passed, but the destruction it had left in its wake was staggering. Villages up and down the coast had been destroyed, some of them completely. Worse, several hundred people had been killed.

As Finneas sat beside Mary in church that

Sunday, he fervently thanked God for the safety they had enjoyed. Only a couple of people from their village had lost their lives. The priest solemnly prayed for their souls. In front of Finneas the town blacksmith, Thomas, bowed his head in sorrow. His wife had been one of those who was lost.

Finneas felt guilty for his and Mary's happiness in the face of so much sorrow. Happy they were, though, for little Pearl sat between them. The storm that had brought her to them had made it easy to explain her sudden presence. They had simply told everyone that she was the child of a distant cousin in another village who had been killed in the storm.

That had satisfied the others, although it hadn't stopped them from casting puzzled looks at Pearl. Finneas closed a hand around Pearl's protectively. Maybe with time the sun would tan her unnaturally pale skin, and as she continued to grow, surely she would grow into her long legs.

She looked up at him with her wide, dark eyes and asked him a question. At least, he thought it was a question. He had no way to answer her, though. Whatever language it was she spoke was foreign to him. He thought it might be Italian, but he wasn't sure.

He just shook his head and squeezed her hand. They were working on teaching her English. He just prayed they would be able to communicate quickly before it became too much of a problem.

Mary turned to look at him and he smiled to hide

his concern. He couldn't help but be afraid. Pearl was different; he wasn't sure how or why, but he did know the people of his village. They didn't tolerate anyone or anything that was different. Only five years earlier an angry mob had seized a woman, a traveling gypsy, accused her of Witchcraft, and burned her at the stake. He shuddered at the memory. *And there was nothing I could do to stop it.*

He gripped Pearl's hand even tighter until she began to wriggle her fingers. He had had a nightmare about the villagers trying to do the same to Pearl and him not being able to reach her. He had awoken screaming and soaked in sweat. He had lied to Mary for the first time in his life, telling her he didn't remember the dream. He had vowed, lying there, shivering and praying, that he would do everything in his power to keep them from hurting Pearl. He just continued to smile at Mary, who had enough to worry about without hearing his fears.

When the services were over, he picked Pearl up in his arms. She hadn't yet seemed to master walking. She was trying, but she just went skittering on her long limbs, wobbling back and forth and landing in a heap time after time. *She just needs to grow into her legs,* he thought.

She wrapped her tiny arms around his neck and looked up at him. She asked him what sounded like a question. Her tiny voice lilted as though she was singing. He just shook his head and kissed her cheek.

She held her pearl out to him and he kissed it as

well. Mary had secured it with a thin piece of rope and a loop so that Pearl could wear the shiny orb around her neck. She laughed up at him. Her laughter, at least, he could understand.

That night Finneas sat bolt upright in bed, awakened by a keening sound that split the stillness and reverberated in the air. Chills danced up and down his spine, and fear touched his heart. Beside him Mary sprang from the bed, grabbing for her shawl. They glanced to the bed where Pearl should have been, but it was empty. A hard knot settled in the bottom of his stomach.

They exchanged frightened glances and began to search the cabin. They found her moments later sitting in the kitchen. She was surrounded by dead fish that were scattered about on the kitchen floor. She must have pulled them off the counter and unwrapped them from their protective coverings.

The stench of death was strong, and an unnatural sound was coming from Pearl. She stared up at them and pointed to a dead fish and then to Finneas. His heart began to pound as he realized that she was blaming him for its death.

Mary knelt down and folded the girl in her arms. "Those are fish. We eat the fish so that we can be strong," she tried to explain.

Pearl began to cry and Mary just held her, clearly not knowing what to say. Finally she looked up at Finneas, and he saw the tears shimmering on her cheeks as well. "Clean up the fish and hide them," she instructed him. "We'll keep them out of her sight, at least for now."

Nodding, Finneas did as he was told. The sound of her cries echoed inside his head continuing long after she had fallen asleep in Mary's arms. It had been a completely unnatural sound, unlike anything he had ever heard.

❖ Chapter Two ❖

Mary came, her face wet with tears, to tell Pearl it was time. Her groom was waiting for her. Pearl began to cry as well, wanting to run, but knowing that she could not.

THIRTEEN YEARS LATER

The hairs on the back of her neck tingled, and Pearl turned her head toward the street. She willed her legs to move forward even as someone beside her cried out. A horse was running out of control, with a cart careening crazily behind him. The owner was chasing behind shouting curses at the beast. Directly in the path of the horse and cart was a small boy playing with a worm he had found in the dirt.

Pearl stumbled but regained her footing. She stretched out her arms and snatched the child, pulling him out of the way. With the child in her arms she tumbled backward and fell, sprawled in the dirt in front of the vegetable cart where she had been shopping.

She lay still for a moment, her heart thudding painfully in her chest. The little boy began to struggle and cry, and his mother rushed to pick him up.

Slowly, Pearl sat up and began to scramble to her feet. She straightened and beat at her skirt, trying to get the dirt out. Realizing it was a futile task, she gave up and picked up her basket from where she had dropped it.

"Thank you for saving him."

Pearl looked up. The child's mother was no older than she was. Pearl wasn't surprised. By the time a young woman from the village reached seventeen, she was usually married and often had at least one child. The little boy was staring at Pearl. Slowly, his arm came up and his finger stretched out, pointing at her.

"You're welcome," Pearl answered. People were staring and she started to fidget uncomfortably.

"Momma," the boy said, still pointing.

"Hush, Samuel."

"But, Momma, look."

Pearl felt tears stinging her eyes as the little boy began gesturing wildly. He strained in his mother's arms as she tried to shush him.

"But Momma, why does she look like that?" he finally shrieked.

Anyone in the village market who had not been staring at the trio before was. The woman whose cart they were standing in front of turned as red as the tomatoes she was selling.

Pearl could feel every pebble in the ground beneath her thin shoes. Like tiny daggers they pierced her feet, rooting her to the spot.

The mother of the child was still trying to hush him, but with little success. She looked at Pearl. "Sorry," she muttered.

But she wasn't sorry. Pearl could tell by the way she stared at her. *She lets her child ask the question that she's too polite to ask herself. Still, they all wonder why I look as I do; they always have.* The other girl turned and hurried off with her son still thrashing about in her arms. The other villagers slowly returned to their shopping, murmuring low as they bent over the various carts arranged around the edge of the village square. Even though Pearl couldn't hear them, she knew they were talking about her.

A chill danced up her spine and she turned to see the blacksmith staring at her. There was something intense in his gaze that unnerved her. She turned around quickly. Shivering, she picked out a tomato, paid for it, and headed for home.

As Pearl walked through the village toward home, she passed the village square. The village square was built around a tall post sticking up from the ground. Ancient traders had erected the post long before the village even existed, as a sign that this place was a crossroads and a good place to meet with other merchants. From those beginnings, people had begun to actually settle near the area of trade and the village had sprung up.

A hundred years earlier, the king of Aster had built the magnificent castle that sat on top of the cliff that towered above the rest of the village. The village itself was on the bottom of the slope. Half of it actually sat on the slant, and the other half on level ground.

On the other side of the village the ground again began to slope, heading down toward the ocean, and a path ran from the village toward the shoreline. It was this path that she walked now. Her father, Finneas, was a fisherman, and she was grateful they lived just outside the village, close to the sea.

Once home, Pearl's shaking hands pulled from her basket the food she had purchased. She removed the tomato and stared at the vibrant red color. It stood out in stark contrast against her pale skin.

She put the tomato away and walked slowly outside. She held her hand up to the light and stared at it. Her skin was so pale, she imagined she could see right through it to the blood and bones beneath. She pulled her braid forward over her shoulders. The hair shimmered against the dark blue of her dress. Her hair, too, was pale, nearly silver.

No wonder the little boy stared. No wonder they whispered. What am I? She stared up at the heavens, but no answer came.

She sighed and began to walk toward the beach, dragging the toes of her shoes. The act of walking to the ocean usually filled her with joy, but her heart was too heavy.

What am I?

When she finally crested the little hill that hid the ocean from her home, she spotted a tall figure staring out to sea. She felt her heart skip a beat as she saw him standing there.

When she was halfway to him, he turned. "There you are!"

She smiled despite herself, wondering how long he had been waiting. His black hair was wildly tousled, indicating that he'd been there quite a while, pacing and thinking. He stood, every inch of his body alert, as though he was a predator poised to pounce on her. *Oh, that he would,* she thought before she could stop herself. Appalled, she pulled her thoughts away from such visions.

James was her best friend, her only friend. She had known him since they were both children, and he was the only one who had never treated her differently because of the way she looked. Perhaps it was because he, too, knew what it was like to be treated differently, to have people whisper and stare, and he disliked it as much as she did.

"Good afternoon, James. How are you?" she asked when she reached his side.

His blue eyes danced, specks of light shimmering in them like whitecaps upon ocean waves. "Impatient. What the devil kept you?"

"Me."

He frowned. "What do you mean by that?"

"I think there's something wrong with me." She sighed, dropping down to sit on the sand.

His eyebrows shot up in surprise, and he took a

seat beside her. "Now, what on earth would make you think that?"

"Look at me! Can you honestly say that anything about me is normal?"

"Normal? Where's the excitement in that?" he snorted. "Besides, who's to say what's normal, anyway?"

"You probably could," she answered.

He waved a hand dismissively. "I would much rather have a life filled with magic than one filled with the mundane."

She couldn't stop herself from laughing. "You are forever searching for magic, James, and I am afraid you shall never find it."

"Well, *you* certainly won't, not with that attitude."

"Good, I have no need of it." The sun beat down upon her skin, and she could feel her tense muscles slowly begin to relax. She breathed deeply and tasted the salty air.

The tide was ebbing, and all along the line of wet sand that the waves had retreated from were little speckles of white shells that had found their way into the shallow water only to be abandoned.

James shook his head at her. "We all need a little magic in our lives, Pearl. We need something to lift us out of our everyday lives and give us something to hope in."

"That's what God is for," she answered defensively.

"Yes, but God is busy. We can't leave it all up to Him."

"Father Gregory would disagree with you."

He snorted. "Father Gregory doesn't believe in anything unless he can see it with his own two eyes or read it in the Bible. Even then I'm not so certain. I think if an angel ever appeared to him he would faint."

"James, how can you be so disrespectful?" she admonished. She was shocked, but also secretly amused. She shouldn't have been surprised. James had had an irreverent streak since she had known him.

He grinned. "I guess it's my birthright."

She couldn't help but blush at that. She dropped her eyes, suddenly too shy to look at him. He noticed the motion, though, and put a hand under her chin. The contact sent tingles along her skin, and when he pushed her head up she found herself pinned by his stare.

"Don't duck your eyes in front of me, Pearl. You know I don't want that."

"Sometimes we do not always get what we want," she answered before she could stop herself.

Her heart stopped for a moment as he stared at her. "I know," he finally answered softly before dropping his hand and looking away. Her heart began to beat again, but now it was pounding so loudly, she was sure he could hear it.

Silence stretched between them and she slowly began to breathe again. They had known each other long enough that the silences were comfortable. Many a time they had sat here for hours not speaking a word, just watching the ocean.

"You know, it was ten years ago today," he said after a moment.

"What was?" she asked.

"That we met," he said, with a short laugh. "Surely you remember."

"How could I forget? I came here to look at the ocean, to be alone with my thoughts, and there was a boy here."

"I was terrified that you were going to tell my father where I was hiding."

"I didn't even know who your father was."

"And I found that so appealing."

"Is that why we're friends?" she teased.

"Well, that and the fact that I found you fascinating."

She remembered the day well, though it seemed but yesterday and not ten years past. He had been so funny that she had laughed nearly the entire time they were together. Even when he had tugged on her hair and told her that it reminded him of the color of the full moon, she hadn't minded somehow. *Maybe it was because he wasn't afraid of me, or judging me.*

"We've been meeting once a week ever since, so over ten years that's about five hundred twenty times."

"Probably more—some weeks we've met twice," she reminded him.

"True," he said, cocking his head to the side as though trying to calculate the exact number.

"What's your point, James?"

He looked at her, suddenly serious. "You know me better than anyone else—sometimes, I think, better than I know myself. I just wanted to say happy anniversary."

She swallowed around the sudden lump in her throat, not knowing what to say. He took her hand and squeezed it gently. A new kind of silence stretched between them, and it was far from comfortable. Her skin prickled as waves of emotion rushed over her.

He broke the silence suddenly enough to startle her. "You want to go for a swim?"

She shook her head, relieved to change the subject. "No, I'll just sit."

"Every week I've asked you and every week you refuse. What is it? Are you shy?"

"No."

"Afraid that I'm a better swimmer? Don't want to be embarrassed?"

"I know you are." She laughed. "I don't swim."

He stared at her. "How can that be? You love the ocean."

"I love to look at it, I don't go in it."

"Well, I'll teach you."

"No!" She winced as she heard the sharp tone in her voice.

He looked shocked. "My father's the only one who's ever taken that tone with me."

"I'm sorry," she mumbled, dropping her eyes. "Forgive me?"

"You know I do." He paused for a moment and then asked, "Why won't you let me teach you?"

She glanced from him to the ocean. She wanted to say yes, to have him take her out into the ocean and teach her to swim. *What would it feel like to have the waters rushing against my skin? And would I ever want to come back? Surely with James by my side I would be safe, he wouldn't let anything happen to me.*

The waves called to her. Below their steady roar and crash there was a singsong voice that she alone seemed to hear. She had tried pointing it out to James and her parents, but none of them heard it. She closed her eyes and listened to it now. The ocean whispered to her, speaking in words that sounded strange and yet achingly familiar to her. *Maybe I'll just put a toe in the water. I could do that.*

She sighed, frustrated, knowing that that wasn't true. She knew that if she put her toe in the water, it wouldn't stop there: Next she would place her whole foot, soon to be followed by the rest of her, and then—then she'd be lost. Forever.

She opened her eyes and looked up at James. He had an expectant look on his face. She shook her head. "I can't go in the water."

"Why not?"

"I just can't," she stammered.

"Why?" he pressed.

"Because if I go in the ocean, I'll die."

He stared at her. "What makes you think that?"

She shook her head, helpless to answer him.

"Did your parents tell you that?"

She shook her head again.

"Do you think that because of what happened when you were little?"

Again, she shook her head. She had no idea where the knowledge had come from, but she was as certain of it as she was her name.

"Tell me again," he whispered, so faint that she could barely hear him.

"What?"

"You know."

Pearl leaned back on the sand. "I've already told you the story, several times."

"Yes, but I enjoy hearing it."

She sighed exaggeratedly. "Okay, but this is the last time." Self-consciously she closed her hand around the black pearl she wore. "Thirteen years ago a fisherman found me in the ocean during a storm. He pulled me into his boat and took home. He and Mary have raised me ever since."

"And all you had with you was that pearl?"

She stroked the dark, shiny orb and nodded.

"And you still have no memory of your life before that?"

"None."

"It is a great mystery."

She grimaced. "I think the only mystery here is why you are so fascinated by the story."

James peered into her eyes. "Look, Pearl. You

might not want to know where you come from, but I do." He leaped back to his feet. "For all we know, you're descended from Fairy folk."

She laughed out loud. "You'd like that, wouldn't you?"

"Well, it would explain your hair."

She felt as though she had frozen inside. He must have seen the look on her face, because he told her, "I know you wish your hair was a different color, brown or red maybe, but I think it's wonderful. Any other color just wouldn't suit you."

He sighed and gazed at the setting sun. A shadow crossed his face, and he looked suddenly older. When he spoke, even the resonance of his voice had deepened slightly. "I should go if I'm to be properly dressed for dinner."

"Who's going to be there tonight?"

He shrugged. "I don't know—a duke, I think."

She grinned. "You don't fool me. Not a person comes or goes at the castle that you don't know who they are and what business they have."

He smiled faintly. "That's true. I just don't like to think about it when I'm with you." He waved his hand to encompass the ocean, the beach, and her. "Here, I don't have to worry about all of that."

She scrambled to her feet and hastened to shake the sand from her skirt. "That's why we do this. So we both can be ourselves. I should go too. I'll see you next week."

"You'll see me tomorrow if you're in the village."

She smiled. "Yes, but then I'll have to call you 'Your Highness.'" She began to walk up the beach away from him.

"You wouldn't have to, you know."

"We both know that's not true," she called back over her shoulder. "You are the prince of Aster, and I am just a fisherman's daughter."

"You don't know that for sure. You might be a princess, for all we know," he shouted.

She waved at him and continued on. "In my dreams. Only in my dreams," she whispered to herself. She heard her father playing the flute, its faint sound tinkling on the wind, and realized that it was later than she had thought. She picked up her skirt and began to run.

Finneas sat outside the cottage. She slowed to a walk as she approached him.

"You're late," Finneas remarked, putting away his flute.

"I'm sorry, Papa."

He raised an eyebrow, but didn't question her.

Pearl slipped past him through the open door into the cottage. For as long as she had lived there, she had only seen the cottage door closed twice during the daytime. Both times it had been shut up against storms. The rest of the time it was open, letting the sea air flood in. For Finneas, the sea provided more than just his livelihood; it was a part of who he was. Mary would sometimes tease that salt water ran through his veins instead of blood.

Inside, Mary glanced at her while stirring the dinner that was boiling in a pot over the fire. "You've been to the beach again."

"How did you know?"

"You've got sand in your hair. What is it you do there, anyway?"

Pearl blushed. "I sit by the water and think."

Looking satisfied, Mary turned back to the table.

Pearl stared at her back for a moment, longing to tell her of the prince and the time they spent together. She opened her mouth to speak, but Finneas came in.

"Everybody wash up," Mary instructed. "I won't have dirty hands at my table."

"Already done," Finneas declared, planting a kiss on his wife's rosy cheek.

Pearl ducked outside and went to the water basin, where she washed her hands and face. It hurt to keep her friendship with James a secret from her parents. Still, she wasn't sure what they would say if they knew. Commoners and royalty didn't speak with one another, everyone knew that. Yet once a week it happened, right on the beach just steps away from her home.

Every week since she was seven, she had met with James. The first time they had met at the oceanside, James had sworn her to secrecy. She had not known who he was, only that he had escaped from some people he called his "keepers." Months later, when she found out he was a prince, she was frightened, for royalty was not supposed to mix with peasants. Still, she had gone to meet him, for he was the only one she could call a friend. Each week he had had to devise more elaborate plans to escape from the castle and his tutors, and she had always laughed until her sides hurt when hearing about his escapades.

The years had passed, though, and eventually there was no longer a need for the secrecy. He was grown up and allowed the freedom to come and go from the castle pretty much as he chose. His father had tried in vain to send personal guards with him, but James always managed to lose them and so his father had at last given up sending them. Still, the meetings had remained their secret. *Of all the secrets in my life, it's the nicest,* she thought.

She went back inside to take her place at the table. Before she reached her chair, though, she caught her foot on the leg of the table and ended up sprawled on the floor. Embarrassed, she scrambled back to her feet. Finneas and Mary were already seated, and she thought she saw Mary suppress a grin.

"Did you trip over your feet again?" Finneas asked dryly.

"No, not mine, this time. It was the table's."

Once she took her seat, they bowed their heads and Finneas began to pray. "Father God, keep us this day. We thank ye for your bounty and pray your forgiveness on us. Bless us and keep us, O Lord. Amen."

They ate in silence. Mary glanced from time to time at Finneas, who stared resolutely at his food. Lost in her own thoughts, it took Pearl several minutes to notice the uncharacteristic silence. She glanced warily toward Mary. The older woman held her gaze for only a moment before averting her eyes. With a mounting sense of unease, Pearl turned to Finneas.

Without looking up from his food, he cleared his throat. "Well, you might as well know. Thomas has been asking about you."

"The blacksmith?"

Finneas nodded affirmatively.

Her stomach began to twist in knots. Something wasn't right. He had been staring at her so strangely in the market. "What does he want?"

Mary began to stand up, but Finneas put a hand on her arm. She locked eyes with her husband, then sank slowly back to her seat.

The silence stretched on for several moments before Mary finally broke it. "He wants to marry you."

"What!"

"He wants to marry you," Finneas affirmed. "He asked me for your hand in marriage this morning."

"What, what did you say?"

Again, a glance between Finneas and Mary. "I told him I would have to think about it."

"Tell him no!"

Finneas sighed heavily and put down his fork. "It would be a good match for you. He's a kind man, and you'd always have a roof over your head and food in your belly."

"He's twice my age."

Finneas muttered something under his breath. "I know that, but it's a good offer and—"

"And what?"

"It's the only one you've had."

Pearl dropped her eyes to her plate as she felt her pale cheeks begin to burn crimson. She should have known this was coming. All of the other girls her age in the village were married. Still, she couldn't stop the feelings of anger and fear that mixed with her shame. "Am I supposed to be grateful, then, that someone would want me? Let me guess: He decided he wanted a wife and he asked after me because I'm the only unmarried woman in the entire village. So, someone had to be desperate to want to marry me?"

Mary quickly put her hand on Pearl's arm. "You know we're not saying that."

"Then what are you saying?"

"It's just that we're not getting any younger, and we won't always be here for you."

"So, I should jump into the arms of the first man to glance my way?"

Finneas shoved back his chair and slammed his fist down onto the table. "By heavens, don't be so stubborn. If a kind man wants you, that should be enough. I didn't see Peter's girl Lizzy complaining when she married the farmer and he was more than twice her age." He turned and strode toward the door. He paused in the threshold long enough to address Mary. "See if you can talk some sense into her." Then he stormed out into the night.

Pearl sat very still, afraid to look at her mother. She had only seen Finneas angry twice before, but never at her. Guilt washed over her. He had been a father to her, raised her as his own. Why couldn't she be a more obedient daughter?

"Well, are you just going to sit there or are you going to say what's on your mind?" Mary asked after a minute.

Tears began streaming down Pearl's face as she looked up. "I don't love him."

"You can learn to love him," Mary said gently. She searched Pearl's face for a minute. "Is there another reason you have? Is there someone you are in love with?"

Pearl's thoughts turned to James. He was her friend and confidant. He was also royalty, though, and beyond her grasp. *Do I love him?* She didn't know, but she thought she might. All she knew of love was what Finneas and Mary showered upon her. But so far as the love between a man and a woman, she knew nothing of it. *Maybe I do love James. Things have been different between us of late. Could that be why I feel strange when I'm around him?* Still, such feelings, if they even existed, would do her no good. "No, Mama, there's no one."

Mary nodded as though it was the answer she was expecting. "Then, daughter, would you at least think about it?"

"It would be good for you and Papa if I said yes, wouldn't it?"

Mary gave a nod so slight that Pearl wasn't even sure she had seen it. "It would be good for you, too. He is a kind man, and you would never want."

"And who else would want someone like me?"

"Any man would be fortunate to have you for a wife."

"Then how come Thomas is the only one asking?" Pearl cried.

Tears shimmered in Mary's eyes as she came around the table and clasped Pearl in her arms.

That night Pearl lay awake, listening to the sounds of the night and wondering what she should do. She resented the choice that had been thrust upon her, though she knew she should be grateful to be given one. Most fathers would never have dreamed of consulting their daughters about a marriage proposal.

I wonder what my real father would have done, she thought, and instantly felt guilty for it. Finneas had been the only father she had known, and she could never have asked for a kinder, more loving father. *Still, there are times when I can't help but wonder what my real parents were like, and what happened to them. I guess I'll never know.*

Her thoughts drifted to James. All his talk about magic and her unknown heritage always pleased her a little. His talk frightened her, though, as well. She wasn't sure she did believe in magic, but she knew that he did, and the thought that it could exist made her nervous. He believed so strongly, though, it was hard not to get swept up by his passion. She thought of the look he got in his eyes when he talked about the things that were near to his heart.

Alone in the dark she could admit that she wished James had been the one who had asked for her hand. She was sure her thoughts must be a sin on her part—pride, presumption, or something. She couldn't quite believe it, though.

James was wonderful, everything that a girl could dream about. He was her dearest friend and she did love him, at least in some sense. Sometimes she dreamt about him at night. He would stand before her and tell her that he loved her, but always, just as he was about to kiss her, she would catch a glimpse of something over his shoulder.

She was never sure what it was, a shadow, perhaps. It was always there, though, and it was somehow familiar to her. It called to her, telling her that there was something else, something she had lost and needed to find. Then, if she strained hard enough, she could see a pair of eyes staring at her, glittering in the darkness.

Those eyes haunted her. She would wake after seeing them, afraid to open her eyes for fear that she would see them blinking at her in the darkness of the cottage. In her dreams James never kissed her, the eyes always stopped him.

The eyes were only in her dreams, never in her

nightmares. The voice in her nightmares was different too. It always whispered horrible things to her, told her she was nothing, nobody. Told her that if she went into the ocean she would die.

Tonight it would be different. Tonight there would be no nightmares. She would dream and she would ignore the eyes, and turn a deaf ear to the whispers. She would dream that she really was a princess, just like James had said.

She rolled over and faced the wall. "If I am a princess, then I shall marry James," she told herself. It was folly, the dream of a girl. Still, the words made her feel better, made her feel like she had a choice. She smiled slightly as she fell asleep.

⁜ Chapter Three ⁜

𝒫rince James walked into the castle. He couldn't help but smile as a servant sweeping the floor only gave him a cursory glance. It used to be that his returns would cause almost as much of an uproar as his disappearances. The alternately happy and frustrating days of childhood had passed, though, and now no one seemed to care whether he came or went. Strangely, he sometimes missed the old days.

He made his way upstairs to his bedchamber. There, a frustrated servant, Peter, was waiting for him. James smiled. At least someone still noticed his comings and goings. His smile faded quickly, though, as Peter promptly began lecturing him on how long it took a gentleman to dress properly for a feast with guests such as the duke and that James should have shown up much earlier and with far less sand upon his person.

With an exaggerated sigh, James sat down on his bed. He surveyed the clothes that had been laid out for him. It was going to be a *very* formal evening. Sir Stephen, the duke of Novan, and his son, Robert, were coming to dinner. James did not trust Sir Stephen. He had met the man thrice before and had disliked him more each time they'd met. "Has Sir Stephen arrived yet?"

Peter wrinkled his nose ever so slightly. James knew the servant did not like the duke any better than he did. Peter also knew more than anyone else about the comings and goings at the castle. If there was news, he would have it.

"He arrived nearly an hour ago with his entourage."

"And?"

"A foul group they are. His servants are an ill-mannered lot. The duke swaggered in like he owned the castle. He doesn't show the proper amount of respect to your lord father."

"And his son? I understand he's earned quite a reputation for himself abroad as a knight."

"More likely he's earned himself a reputation as a scoundrel."

James couldn't suppress a laugh. "Has Father said anything?"

Peter shook his head. "Your father has his mind on other matters. He doesn't notice Sir Stephen's insolence."

"But you think he should?"

Peter dropped his eyes. "It is not my place to say what your father should do."

"And yet, you will," James pushed.

Peter paused for a moment, and James leaned forward eagerly. When Peter spoke, it was in a hushed whisper. "I think your father should watch him close.

The duke's an ambitious man, and I wouldn't put much stock in his scruples."

"But he is my father's distant cousin," James protested.

"And as such would take the throne if something happened to your father, and to you."

James felt a shiver dance up his spine. Although Peter was in touch with all that happened around the castle, he was not given to idle gossip. If he said a thing, it was gospel.

James kept his own voice low as he answered, "Then I shall keep an eye on the duke for my father's sake."

He extended his hand to Peter, and after a moment the servant clasped it. They locked eyes, and a silent agreement passed between them. They would keep an eye on the duke.

Peter released his hand, and James stood up. "Well, it's time to dress for dinner. We mustn't keep Father and the duke waiting."

"No, Your Highness."

In short order, James was properly attired. What would Pearl say about his clothes? They were more elaborate than any she had ever seen him in. On the couple of occasions that she had actually seen him in the village, he had worn simpler clothes, still regal, but not like those he wore when they were holding court.

He hoped she would laugh and call him a gilded peacock, or smile and tell him he looked handsome.

More likely, though, she would duck her head and refuse to look at him, unable to forget his station—or hers.

She was so beautiful, and yet she did not know it. There was something ethereal about her, as though she were from a different world. When they were young he used to dream that she was a fairy, or a spirit who would one day disappear into thin air. Now that they were older, he didn't know what to believe. He wasn't sure he believed in Fairy folk anymore, but he wasn't entirely convinced they weren't real. There were too many stories, too many unexplained happenings. The only thing he knew for sure was that there was more to Pearl than she herself knew.

He met his father as he walked out of his chamber. King Philip nodded at him. Together they walked down the winding staircase that led to the main floor and the great hall. They crossed the threshold, and everyone inside the hall, including Sir Stephen, rose to their feet.

It looked like there would be nearly fifty people dining with them tonight. Aside from the duke and his son there were knights, merchants, and a few other, lesser nobles. James and his father arrived at the table and took their place at its head. James noted that Peter was standing in his usual place, just behind and to the right of the king, in case he should need anything.

Everyone else sat down on the long benches on the sides of the table. A massive stone fireplace that ran nearly the length of the one wall cast light and heat into the room. A hanging candelabra above the center of the table and long taper candles placed at intervals down the center of the table provided the rest of the light.

As soon as they were seated, the servants appeared as if by magic, filling each cup with clarrey, a wine that James knew his father favored, with its mix of honey and spices. Then, serving maids from the kitchens appeared carrying trays of meats, fruits, and other delicacies. The aroma filled the room, and James breathed deep, enjoying the mixture of scents.

There were trays of spiced pear compote and plates of exotic fruits. There were legs of mutton and vegetables in vinegar. Flampoyntes were set before each guest, the pork and cheese pies decorated with pastry triangles. Various other meats and cheeses were present in abundance.

There was Sweet William, the fish that Pearl had shown him once that usually smelled of ammonia. Most wouldn't eat it, but their chef prided himself on having perfected a way to cook it that removed the odor. The result was a succulent dish that had an exotic flavor. James smiled to himself. Finneas was the only fisherman who caught Sweet William and he did so only for the castle's chef. It made James feel close to Pearl, somehow, to sit at his father's table and eat the fruits of her father's labor.

The most decadent dish was brought out last with a great flourish. Whole roasted chickens graced great serving platters. Each was stuffed with meat, nuts, eggs, and spices and were glazed either green or gold. Balls of the stuffing were shaped like eggs around each chicken and were also painted either green or gold.

Gasps of appreciation went up around the table at the sight of the poullaille farcie, and James sighed in satisfaction. In his experience nothing was quite so impressive as a table laid with such exquisite food. He knew from his tutors that the meal was a symbol of the king's wealth and power, and should serve to humble the hearts of those present. His eyes turned to the duke. Even Sir Stephen was impressed; James could see it in the way his eyes were riveted upon the chickens. James would have to remember to thank the chef later.

For half an hour the only sound was that of hungry men eating. Not for the first time since his mother had died five years before, James lamented a lady's touch at the table. His father had never remarried, and the only women who had sat at the table in the past five years had been the occasional wife of a visiting noble or a distant relative visiting the family.

James's thoughts again drifted to Pearl. He wondered what she'd be eating at her family's table. *Not fish*, he thought wryly. Even he knew of her distaste for the sea's bounty. He imagined her sitting at the table beside him. What would she try first? He yearned to have her dine with him. He had never been able to even show her the castle, though. He felt his cheeks burning with shame. For all her talk about the difference in their stations and her reluctance to speak with him in public, he was just as bad. He had never even spoken her name in front of his father.

"So, Prince James is of an age to take a bride."

Startled, James looked up from his plate and stared at Sir Stephen.

King Philip nodded slowly. "Yes, he is."

"I imagine there are any number of eligible ladies eager to be his wife. It must be hard to choose between them." The duke picked up his goblet and took a swallow. He set it back down on the table and with exaggerated nonchalance continued. "I have had several requests from young suitors for the hand of my own daughter, Elizabeth."

James glanced uneasily at his father. He noted that the king was looking at Peter. Peter shook his head ever so slightly, and the king turned back to face the duke.

James wasn't sure what the interchange between Peter and his father meant, but he didn't want to risk finding out. He didn't like where the conversation seemed to be headed. "I'm sure one of them will make a fine husband for your daughter," he spoke up quickly. "Having them be the supplicants for her hand puts her in a position of power, and you, as well," he added pointedly.

The duke flushed. James had touched a nerve. If the duke asked another to wed his daughter, it would put him in the weaker position, that of supplicant.

The duke was sensitive enough to the subtleties of power to appreciate the difference, and to not enjoy being reminded of it. James was relieved. There would be no talk of his betrothal tonight at least.

James turned his head away from the duke and caught sight of Robert, who had been quiet up until now, smiling wickedly. The smile did nothing to alleviate the crackling cold of his gray eyes. James met his eyes and was startled to see arrogance, rage, and hatred lurking in their crystal depths. A shiver slid up his spine.

During the rest of the meal James was quiet, watching and, in turn, being watched. It was unnerving and it was with relief that he excused himself at the end of the meal.

He quickly climbed the stairs leading to the living quarters, eager to be alone with his thoughts. Inside his room he strode to the window and stared out toward the sea and Pearl's home.

Of late he had found himself thinking more and more about her and often at the strangest times. Things were changing between them, in some subtle way that was hard to detect and even harder to understand. *Maybe we've just grown up, and this is what it will feel like from now on.*

He didn't know how long he'd been standing there before he heard a slight noise behind him. He turned around to see Peter standing a respectful distance away. "What is it, Peter?"

"Your father wishes to speak with you."

"What about?" James asked, at once suspicious and curious.

Peter just shrugged.

"Don't know or won't tell?"

The ghost of a smile touched Peter's lips. "Perhaps a bit of both. He's in the throne room." With that, he turned and left, and James found his curiosity heightened even more.

He left his chambers and made his way toward the throne room—further proof that whatever it was had to be somewhat serious, else they would have met in his father's chambers. When he reached the room he found his father standing, staring out a window, much as James had just been doing upstairs. Silently James joined him, and together they stared out into the darkness.

Without turning toward him, his father spoke. "You did well in speaking to the duke tonight. You discouraged him from his purpose and saved him the embarrassment of rejection."

"I couldn't marry his daughter."

King Philip turned to look at him. "You've met her?"

"No, I'm sure she's a lovely young lady. It's her father I have a problem with."

The king nodded. "So I noticed."

"I don't trust him, Father. There's something insincere about him."

"As opposed to all the courtiers?" his father asked with a faint smile.

James couldn't help but smile back. "I see your

point. Speaking frankly for a moment, though, I think the duke is dangerous."

His father put a hand on his shoulder. "Leave the duke for me to worry about. You need to be concerning yourself with other matters."

"What?" James asked cautiously.

"Marriage. The duke was right about that, at least. It's time you take a bride."

James pulled back. "But, Father!"

"No, I've left you alone for a long time—too long. It's my fault. I wanted you to enjoy your life before you had to take up the burden of your position. Well, the time has long past come. You need to step up to your responsibilities as prince and future king of Aster. And the first responsibility you must take up is getting married. In this I am immovable."

"But . . . who?"

"On that question I am a little more flexible. Do you know why I never remarried?"

The question caught James off guard. He shook his head.

His father's voice dropped to a whisper. "Because I truly loved your mother. We two were fortunate, more so than most others. I would wish that kind of happiness for you."

James didn't know what to say. Naked pain danced in King Philip's eyes. After a moment, he continued in a husky voice.

"I'm prepared to help you in whatever way I can. I could throw a ball and invite all the eligible ladies of this kingdom and the surrounding ones to attend. . . ."

James wrinkled his nose. "No, thank you, Father. I think I just have to figure this out for myself."

"Well, whatever you're going to do, do it quickly, else I shall be forced to choose for you."

"And who would you choose?"

"The Lady Elaine."

The Lady Elaine was six years James's senior and still unmarried, with good reason. The lady had a pleasant face and a nice form, but it was when she opened her mouth that others fled. It wasn't just that she had a voice that brayed like a mule, it was that with her word choice she more often resembled that creature than any other. She was not only prone to saying the wrong thing at the wrong time, she was also critical of everything, and her opinion was freely shared with all.

"Oh Father, anyone but her!" James protested.

The king raised an eyebrow. "Really? You would prefer the duke's daughter?"

"No," James answered quietly.

His father nodded once and then turned to stare back out the window. The interview was over. James stood only a few moments more before leaving quietly. He was sure that his muted footsteps on the floor were completely drowned out by the pounding of his heart.

Peter was entering his chamber with a fresh pitcher of water when James arrived back there. The older man lifted an eyebrow upon seeing him. James threw himself on the bed as Peter placed the pitcher on a table across the room.

"Will there be anything else, Your Highness?"

James sighed as he glanced at Peter. The servant had always been a friend and confidant, something of a second father to him.

"He wants me to marry."

Peter didn't say anything.

"You knew that's what he wanted to speak with me about, didn't you?"

"I had my suspicions."

"What am I going to do? All the princesses and noble ladies I've met have bored me to tears. I can't imagine happiness trapped in a marriage with one of them."

"I'm sure there are other possibilities."

"Who?"

"What about your little friend from the village?"

James felt the color drain from his face as he sat upright. "How do you know about her?"

Peter actually laughed. "Highness, please, I've known about her for years."

"My father?"

"Knows nothing about her. Still, I think he would understand. Your mother was not your grandfather's first choice for a daughter-in-law."

"Yes, but she was from a noble family." James shook his head. "This is insanity, anyway. Pearl is my best friend."

Peter raised an eyebrow. "Many marriages have been based on less than that."

"Do you really think Father would approve?"

"He might and he might not. The thing is, though, he's not so much eager that you have a wife as that you have an heir."

James nodded. "I figured that was what he was thinking. He was just being polite by not mentioning 'bride' and 'child' in the same sentence." He looked at Peter. The older man was possessed of keen insight, not only into people, but also into situations and events.

"What would you do?" James asked.

Peter looked at him kindly. "I'd follow my heart."

The next morning watery sunlight shone through James's window. He had barely slept all night, falling asleep in the dark hour before the dawn. The only thing he was sure about was that he had to talk to Pearl, and soon.

His clothes had already been laid out for him, and he dressed quickly. He hoped he would see Pearl when he went to the village. He grimaced. Even if he was able to see her, talking to her would prove a different challenge.

When he entered the Hall, he found Robert eating breakfast alone. The marquis looked up, stood, and bowed. James nodded and kept walking. He was in no mood for idle chatter.

"Highness, if I may have a moment of your time."

James groaned and considered what would happen if he just kept walking. He measured the distance to the door and wondered if he could feign deafness. He had vowed to keep an eye on the duke, though, and that included watching his son. He turned and smiled weakly. "What is it, Robert?"

"I was actually wanting your advice on something."

James's eyebrows shot up in surprise. He wouldn't have thought that Robert would want his advice on anything. Intrigued, he asked, "What about?"

"Women. Or, to be more precise, one woman."

Now James was really bewildered. "Go on."

"I have fallen in love with a young lady and I wanted to ask her father for her hand in marriage."

"A noble endeavor. Where does the difficulty lie?"

"The lady in question is common born—a peasant, to put it bluntly."

"I see," James replied slowly. "And you're worried about marrying her and the possible repercussions?"

"Yes, Highness, I am."

"Do you love her?" James asked, privately astonished that he and Robert should have more in common than he would have thought.

"I do."

"Then do not worry. My father might not be happy, but he will not block your union with this woman."

"Your father has always seemed to me to be very benevolent, and respectful of all, regardless of their station," Robert noted.

"Yes, he is," James answered, smiling. "I've always admired him for that."

"As is to be expected. Now, if my own father will prove as understanding, all should be well."

"I shall pray for understanding from both of our fathers," James remarked, knowing Robert could not know he would be asking it for them both. James nodded his head. "I will see you at dinner."

Robert bowed, and James headed for the door. Once he reached it he turned back around. "Robert, when you have proposed to your lady, bring her back to the castle so that she might prepare adequately for your wedding."

"You are too gracious, Your Highness," Robert said, bowing once more.

Smiling, James left the room. If he could help Robert, he must be able to help himself.

❧ Chapter Four ❧

Pearl reached the doors of the church, her steps halting and her heart hammering in her chest like a frightened bird. Tears fell on the flowers she carried in her hand. It was supposed to be good luck for the bride to cry. Pearl was afraid, though, that no amount of luck could save her.

Pearl stood at the fruit cart, trying hard to ignore the fact that she was only a stone's throw away from the blacksmith's forge. She tried to pretend she couldn't hear Thomas's booming voice as he greeted passersby. It wasn't working. Chills danced up her spine.

"Well, are you going to buy something or just stand there gawking?" asked the lady minding the cart.

Pearl jumped and muttered an apology. She hurriedly picked out what she wanted, filled her basket with fruit, and paid for it. She started to turn, wishing to be away from the blacksmith. A stone twisted under her foot, though, and she fell headlong, apples spilling out across the ground in front of her. Stunned, she lay for a moment, willing the earth to open and swallow her.

"Pearl, are you all right?"

She looked up to see Thomas staring down at her. She felt herself flush as he offered his hand. She took it reluctantly and scrambled back to her feet. He stooped and retrieved the apples and handed them back to her. His fingers brushed hers, and she jerked involuntarily.

"I've been wanting to talk with you, Pearl." He shifted his weight from foot to foot and stared intently at her.

She opened her mouth to say something, anything, to keep him from continuing. Nothing came to mind.

"Make way for Prince James!"

The herald's cry saved her. Thomas turned to look and to back out of the way of the royal entourage. Pearl took the opportunity to slip away. She dashed through the crowd, praying to go unnoticed. She stopped only when she had put a good distance between her and Thomas.

As she paused to calm herself, she caught sight of James coming toward her. Dressed in finery and wearing a cloak of rich velvet, he looked so different than he did when in the simple clothes she normally saw him in. As he drew abreast of her she bowed like everyone else. After all, he might be her friend, but he was her prince first and foremost.

He paused almost imperceptibly in front of her and cast a sideways glance. "Meet me after dinner," he instructed, his voice so low, she scarcely heard him.

She dipped her head in understanding. Her heart

was in her throat. Never before had he risked speaking to her in public, and rarely had he asked to meet on a different day. Then he swept on, followed by guards, attendants, and the curious. Once they had passed, she made her way through the crowd and headed for home.

She was halfway there before her heart stopped pounding.

Inside the cottage she found Mary preparing a goose. Pearl grinned at the thought of the coming dinner. Mary looked up from her work and waved a finger at her. "I see you smiling. It's scandalous that a fisherman's daughter prefers goose to fish."

"I can't help it. I feel sorry for the poor little fish."

"And not the goose?" Mary shook her head. "You've always been a strange one, Pearl."

"Why, Mama?"

"Why what?"

Pearl swallowed hard. "Why am I so different from everyone else?"

Mary's brow furrowed. "You're not, dear. I didn't mean it that way."

"No, this isn't about the goose. It's about everything . . . my hair, my skin, my legs."

Her mother didn't look up, and appeared to be very intent on her preparations. The way she began to hack at the goose with a knife was erratic, though, a sign of strain. "What's wrong with your legs?"

"Nothing, if I were a horse."

"They're just . . . a little long."

"They're very long, they don't fit with the rest of me, and I'm constantly tripping over my feet."

"You'll grow into them," Mary hastened to reassure her.

"Mama, I'm seventeen. I think I'm done growing."

"Pearl, there is nothing wrong with you. My mother had skin nearly as pale as yours, and the baker's children in the next village all have light, whitish hair."

"And the legs?" she asked gloomily.

"Some people have big hands, large noses. Your father has huge feet—even the cobbler says so. So, you have long legs. There's nothing wrong with that."

"I guess," Pearl whispered, unconvinced. She took a breath and pressed further. "Where do you think I came from?"

"My, you're full of questions today."

"Haven't you ever wondered?"

Mary set the goose down hard and stared into Pearl's eyes. "No, I haven't. You were a gift from God, a child He wanted to be protected, and that was all I ever needed to know. You worry too much, Pearl."

Pearl nodded, recognizing the tone in Mary's voice and knowing there was no use trying to talk to her more about it. *It has to be painful for her when I ask such things, a reminder that she's not my birth mother.* A wave of remorse swept over her. "I'll go wash up so I can help you."

"Pearl." Mary's voice trembled slightly. "I love you.

I couldn't love you any more even if I'd given birth to you. Sometimes I think I love you more because I didn't. You are the most precious gift I ever received. We want only your happiness."

"I know, Mama," Pearl answered softly.

The rays of the setting sun seemed to touch the ocean. Pearl knew that she should probably be getting home, but James still hadn't said a word, just paced up and down the sand. Her eyes followed him as the fading sunlight danced across his black hair. He must have come straight from dinner. He was still dressed in all his castle finery, and it unnerved her a little. Sometimes she almost imagined that he was two different people: the prince of Aster, and her friend James.

"How was your day?"

She jumped at his voice and laughed shakily. "Well, I embarrassed myself in the marketplace and had to face Thomas."

"Thomas?" His brow furrowed in thought. "You mean the blacksmith?"

"Yes."

"I'm afraid I don't understand. Was he cruel to you?"

"No." She took a deep breath. "Last night my father told me that Thomas had asked for my hand in marriage."

"What! He's like a hundred years older than you!"

She couldn't help but laugh at his exaggeration. "I know."

"You refused, of course."

She hesitated long enough that he spun around and locked eyes with her. She sighed. "It's not that simple, I'm afraid."

"Of course it is. You just say no. That's all there is to it."

"No, that's not all. If I am to be a dutiful daughter, I should accept. He is . . . a kind man and I . . . I would always be provided for."

James's eyes narrowed and he pursed his lips. He stared at her long and hard, and it unnerved her. She wanted to look away but couldn't; there was something in his eyes that shot through her. He stepped close to her suddenly. "Is Finneas forcing you into this?" he asked, grasping her upper arms.

"No. I know he thinks I should accept, though," she answered, shaken by his intensity.

James barked a short laugh. "Ha, you can do much better than Thomas."

Pearl felt tears welling up in her eyes. "Look at me, James."

He did, staring deeply into her eyes. His hands still grasped her arms, and she realized with a shiver just how close he was standing to her. Another step and she would be in his arms.

She swallowed hard, forcing herself to continue. "All the other girls my age are married. Thomas is the first one to ask for my hand . . . and there won't be any others."

He released her and stepped back. "Of course

there will be," he said, with the ease of someone always surrounded by possibilities and a variety of choices.

It was moments like this when she felt how different they really were. Any woman would gladly marry a prince; James could have anyone he wanted. She, on the other hand, was just the daughter of a poor fisherman, with a strange appearance and dismal prospects. Frustration welled up inside her. "Look at me! Who else would want a wife who looks so strange and who is constantly tripping over her own feet? Nobody, that's who! It's not like I'm royalty that I can pick and choose whomever I want. I'm lucky my father even took my feelings into consideration."

She burst into tears, unable to contain her frustration and anger any longer. She sank down upon the sand, and he dropped down beside her. They sat for several minutes, her crying and him letting her. When at last her tears began to dry, he put a hand under her chin and pulled her head up. When she met his eyes, she saw tears in them.

"Pearl. It is not so easy for royalty, either. Last night my father told me he wanted me to marry. He suggested a princess I barely know and cannot much tolerate. Still, it would be a good political alliance for Aster. He has not said that I must marry her, but he has made it clear that I must marry quickly. I think he wants to see a grandson before he dies."

Pearl's heart sank as a fresh wave of tears burst forth. James reached out and gripped her hand with his. His fingers entwined with hers, and the intimacy of the touch startled her and sent ripples of shock through her and stemmed the flow of tears. "Pray that God gives me wisdom, and I shall pray to discover how I might help you," he whispered.

Pearl could only nod, her mouth having gone dry. His thumb was tracing a path across the back of her hand.

With his free hand he reached out and touched the pearl around her neck. His fingers brushed against her skin. "You are incredibly special, Pearl. Do not agree to marry the blacksmith."

She nodded, not trusting herself to speak.

He took a deep breath. "We should both get back before we're missed. Do you need me to walk you home?"

She didn't know what to say. James had never before offered to walk her home. For one brief moment she wondered what her parents would think if she showed up on the arm of the prince. *They would probably be appalled to find out about our clandestine meetings conducted without the benefit of a chaperone.*

"No, I can manage," she muttered.

They rose to their feet, he still clasping her hand. "Pearl, everything will be all right."

"For you as well."

His fingers lingered on hers as they pulled away from each other. She watched him walk quickly away until he was lost to her sight. She stood, rubbing wonderingly the hand that he had held. Ten years and he had never held her hand like that. *What made him start now?*

In the morning Pearl had trouble meeting Mary's eyes across the table. She had barely slept, her emotions being in such turmoil. She wasn't very hungry, and the aroma of boiling fish was making her nauseated.

"Hello in there!" a voice called from outside the cabin. Pearl jumped as Mary and Finneas looked at each other in bewilderment. They rarely received visitors, and none this early.

"Hello, yourself!" Finneas boomed as he started to stand.

A figure darkened the doorway, and Pearl caught her breath as she recognized James. He was without his finery, wearing only the simple clothes he normally did for their walks on the beach.

"I hope I have not disturbed the house," James said.

His face was a study in innocence as he said it. It was a ridiculous sentiment, though. Given the time of morning it would have been impossible for a peasant not to disturb the house, let alone the prince of Aster. For a moment there was shocked silence as Finneas and Mary realized who he was.

"Your Highness!" Mary gasped, rising and curtsying.

Finneas bowed deeply. "You honor us with your presence. Would you care to sit, milord?"

Pearl felt an urge to start laughing. It was unreal seeing him standing there in her home in front of her parents. All the times she had agonized over wanting to tell them about her friendship with him, and yet she had always felt compelled to keep silent. Now he strode in as nonchalant as though he had breakfast there every morning.

Mary suddenly noticed that Pearl hadn't risen to pay respect to their prince. "Pearl," she hissed. "Greet our guest."

A smile twisting her face, Pearl complied. She rose to her feet, curtsied nicely, and said, "Good morning, James."

Mary and Finneas both gasped at her familiarity. She had to bite her tongue to keep from laughing. She sank back down into her chair, her legs feeling weak.

James was grinning from ear to ear. "Good morning, Pearl. I trust you slept well."

The familiarity of the question made her blush. He had asked her such things before, but never in the presence of others.

She drew a shaky breath. "Horribly, and you?"

"About the same, I'm afraid."

Mary and Finneas stared back and forth between the two, horror and disbelief mingling on their faces.

"Good sir, I believe I will take you up on that offer of a seat," James said.

Finneas hastened to bring a chair to the table for him, and he took it with grace.

"Would you like breakfast, my lord?" Mary asked.

"Only if everyone else is still eating."

It was settled. Mary and Finneas slowly reclaimed their seats after setting a plate of food before him. They picked up their own forks, but didn't eat, just continued to stare.

Pearl had no idea what James was up to, but she was sure that if she let herself laugh she would never stop. The secret of their friendship would now be known to her parents, and although the thought made her a little sad, it mostly brought her relief.

James attacked his food with gusto, and Pearl wondered if he had skipped breakfast or was just being polite. "This is wonderful. You are an excellent cook."

"Thank you, my lord," Mary stammered.

After he had consumed half his food, James put his fork down. "I suppose you are wondering why I am here."

"The thought had crossed our minds," Finneas answered.

"I have some things I need to discuss with Pearl this morning."

"With . . . Pearl?" Mary asked wonderingly.

James nodded. "You see, for years she has been my friend and loyal adviser. I can tell from your shocked faces that she has never told you of this. Please do not blame her, for she was only doing as I asked. I swore her to secrecy years ago and I am greatly impressed that she has kept her word."

Pearl glanced at her father's astounded look and nodded. James's smile only grew broader.

Realization dawned in Mary's eyes. "When you are walking on the beach?"

"Just on Tuesdays," Pearl quickly told her. "At least, normally."

"Why Pearl?" Finneas questioned.

"The best reason in the world. She is a good listener. Also, she doesn't have any notions about what a prince should and shouldn't do—at least not until recently. She always shows me a fresh perspective. At any rate, I came by this morning because I need her advice and it cannot wait until next week. I decided that it was time to meet you as well, since there is no longer truly a need to keep our meetings a secret."

He laughed. "It's funny. I feel like I already know you both. I've seen you both before, and Pearl has told me so much about you and has been such a large part of my life for so many years that I feel as though I know you."

"I wish we could say the same," Mary said with a weak smile.

For a moment there was silence at the table. Pearl clasped her hands in her lap, trying to hide their shaking. "When he was little he used to sneak out of the castle and he didn't want anyone knowing where he was going," she explained.

"Three hours of freedom once a week isn't too much to ask for a child, is it?" James questioned.

"No," Finneas hastened to reassure him. "It must be horrible for a child not to have any time to himself to play, to constantly be watched over, and to be cooped up."

James smiled. "I should have had you speak with my father years ago."

It was Finneas's turn to flush red and drop his eyes.

"So, would it be all right if I borrow Pearl for the day? I promise I'll have her back by late afternoon."

Mary and Finneas exchanged glances. Finally Finneas spoke. "We would be honored to have our daughter advise you, Your Highness."

"Wonderful! Now, let's finish our breakfast, shall we?"

The rest of the meal was eaten in the same awestruck silence. It was just as well, for Pearl's thoughts were far too many to allow her to speak coherently. *What could James want to talk about that couldn't wait?* It had to be drastic to bring him here. She felt sure that it had something to do with both their impending betrothals, but she wished she knew what it was.

When everyone had finished eating, James pushed back from the table and rose to his feet. "Thank you for your kind hospitality."

"Should I send a midday meal with you, my lord?" Mary asked as she stood.

"That would be wonderful. Thank you."

"Thank you for honoring our home with your presence," Finneas replied.

James's smile vanished and his voice was sincere as he answered, "It is an honor for me to be here and to meet the people who have raised and sheltered my friend."

While Mary quickly put together some bread and cheese, Pearl braided her hair and put on her shoes. She finished just in time for Mary to hand her a bundle.

"I hope it's enough," Mary whispered with a worried frown.

Knowing Mary's tendency to provide more food than was needed, Pearl squeezed her hand. "I'm sure it will be fine."

After James said good-bye to Mary and Finneas, he and Pearl headed out the door and walked quickly toward the beach. The day was warm and fair, and Pearl breathed in deeply, filling her lungs with the salty air.

"Well, that went well," James commented, his face expressionless.

Pearl laughed. "I cannot believe you did that."

"Are you sorry that I did?"

"I guess not. It just feels odd."

"There's no going back now."

It was a strange comment, and when she glanced at him she saw a gleam in his eyes. She decided to let it drop as the beach came into sight. A small, dark object stood out against the light sand, and Pearl craned her neck trying to see what it was.

It looked like a boat, and disappointment washed over her. *Of all the days for someone to show up on our beach!*

James picked up speed and headed straight for the boat. "I thought we might actually go out on the water today instead of just sit by it," he said, glancing at her.

Fear wrapped itself around her heart and began to squeeze. "I . . . I don't think that's a good idea," she stammered.

"It's a wonderful idea. If I can't get you to go into the water, I can at least get you out on the surface. And, technically, since you won't be *in* the ocean so much as *on* it, you'll be safe." He smiled. "I'll keep you safe, I promise."

She looked back at him with wide eyes. "Well, this is a day of surprises."

"That's the plan," he answered cryptically.

He took her hand and pulled her toward the boat. Her heart skipped a beat at his touch even as she struggled to make sure she didn't trip. Once they reached the boat, Pearl deposited the bundle of food in it.

"You get in and I'll push the boat out into the water," James instructed.

"Should I help?" she asked, terrified that he might say yes. She hadn't so much as put a foot in the ocean since the night Finneas had found her.

"No, a lady should not have to get her feet wet."

"I'm not a lady. I'm just me, Pearl," she protested.

"I thought we'd been through this already. We really do not know who or what you are."

"But—"

He held up a hand to silence her protests. "No. Today, Pearl, you are a lady, a princess, and someday the whole world shall know it."

She scrambled into the boat. Once seated, she tried to tuck her skirt around her and sit up straight. If he wanted her to be a princess, couldn't she at least pretend for a little while? *It's just the two of us; what harm can it do?*

He pushed the boat into the water and once it was a few feet out, he hopped in and began to row. Still struggling to pretend that she was a princess, Pearl bit her lip to keep from offering to help again.

James kept rowing until the little boat was quite a distance out from the shore and the water was peaceful. At last he stopped rowing and secured the oars. Leaning back, he closed his eyes and breathed in deeply.

For a long time neither of them spoke. Pearl stared down into the water, watching all the shifting colors of blue and green and wishing as she had many times before that she could dive beneath the surface and explore the depths of the sea. What secrets would she find there?

"What are you thinking?" he asked at last.

She looked up to see his blue eyes studying her intently.

She shrugged. "Silly thoughts."

"Tell me."

"I was just wishing that I could dive down and swim with the fish, see their world."

He nodded as though it was the most natural wish in the world. He always seemed to understand her. For one wild moment Pearl wondered what it would truly be like to spend her life with him. She dropped her eyes, afraid he might read something in them that she did not wish him to know.

He did not let her retreat, though. He leaned forward. "Pearl, look at me."

She complied reluctantly.

"You always duck your eyes when you talk to me and I hate it. Is it because I am a prince or are you hiding something from me?"

She felt a guilty flush creep up her throat, and her cheeks began to burn.

"I mean sometimes I think I know everything there is to know about you, and other times you seem like a stranger to me."

"Sometimes I seem like a stranger to me too," she admitted.

He shook his head and sighed. "Well, that's not what I wanted to come out here to talk to you about."

"What did you want to talk about?" she asked, her heart beginning to beat faster.

"I think I have a solution to our problems."

"Really?"

"Yes," he said. His eyes grew soft, and he took her right hand in his. "Pearl we've known each other for a long time, and you are my best friend."

"And you are mine."

He squeezed her hand and stared into her eyes.

"There's something I want to tell you." He leaned toward her, and she held her breath.

"What is it?"

Suddenly his eyes went wide and he seemed to be staring at something just behind her. "We've sprung a leak."

For a moment she wasn't sure what he had said, and then it hit her as she felt cold water seeping into her shoes. She looked down to see the bottom of the boat rapidly filling with water. She turned and saw it bubbling up between a crack in the wood on the floor behind her. Quickly she scooped up the bundle of food and pulled off the outer cloth. She tried plugging the crack with it even as James picked up the oars and began to row.

"There's nothing to use to bale out the water," he called to her.

She nodded grimly as the water kept seeping in. She tore some cloth from the bottom of her skirt and continued to try to stop up the leak, but it was no use. The water was creeping past her ankles, and the boat was sitting lower and lower in the water. She could feel herself panicking. *I'm not safe, I'm not safe,* she kept thinking over and over as the water lapped at her legs. "It's not working," she finally said, turning toward James.

He nodded grimly and pointed toward the shore. They had made a lot of progress, but it was still quite a ways off. "I'll get us as close as we can, and then we'll have to swim for it."

"No, the water . . . I can't!"

"Pearl, I will not let anything happen to you. I'm a strong swimmer, and together we will make it back to shore. Trust me."

"Is this another one of your surprises?"

He gave a sound that was half laugh, half grunt as he continued to strain at the oars. "Afraid I can't take credit for this one. This is definitely not how I envisioned this boat ride ending."

She tried to stop herself from imagining how he had wanted it to end. There would be time enough for that later. Still, her heart was racing and she wasn't at all sure the sinking boat was the cause.

"You going to be okay with your heavy skirt?" he asked as the water crept up her calves.

"I'll manage."

"Okay, relax and you'll be all right. Jump away from the boat so it won't pull you under when it sinks. Kick with your legs and move your arms back and forth like you're grabbing something in front of you and pulling it toward you. I'm going to be right behind you. Just shout if you get in trouble. We've only got a few more seconds. Get ready to jump."

She nodded and poised herself. Terror wrapped its icy hand around her heart and began to squeeze. He abandoned the oars and stood up beside her. "On the count of three. Ready? One, two, three!"

Pearl jumped as far away from the boat as she could. She hit the water and a second later heard another splash as James joined her. She panicked and flailed her arms about wildly. She started to cough violently as water entered her nose and mouth. What had James told her? *Relax.* As she bobbed up and down in the water, she thought, *I should have let him teach me to swim. I wish I could swim.*

She stopped flailing wildly and began to move her arms back and forth rhythmically. She made a little bit of headway. *James was right.* He had been right about her skirt, though, too. Wet, it weighed so much more and slowed her down. She kicked free of her shoes and that at least helped. Focusing on the land, she started to kick.

The water became more rough the closer she got to the shore. She started to panic again, but a memory stirred. She had once seen James carried into shore by cresting waves, riding on their peaks on his stomach. She fixed the memory in her mind, studying it, remembering the way he had started to move just a second before the wave hit him.

The waves began to crash around her and she swallowed seawater. Her arms and legs felt as if there were dead weights attached to them. As she turned, she spied a large wave coming that she judged would make it all the way to the beach. Moments before it reached her she started to swim again. The wave caught her and lifted her up. It carried her all the way to the beach and she ended up on the sand, where she coughed and gasped for air.

She crawled farther up the beach, away from the waves crashing around her, and then finally collapsed.

She lay for a minute, catching her breath and gathering her strength. *I'm alive!* she thought. Relief and gratitude flooded through her as she grabbed fistfuls of sand and let it run through her fingers. Finally she struggled to her feet.

"James, we made it," she called. She moved her hand to her throat to stroke her pearl and reassure herself that she hadn't lost it in the ocean. It was warm to her touch, but as her fingers twisted about it, it slowly regained its coolness.

There was no reply, and she glanced down the beach in either direction. Nothing. Panic began to swell in her as she cast her eyes back toward the sea. There was nothing, no dark figure, not even the remnants of their boat.

James was gone.

❧ Chapter Five ❧

$\mathcal{D}$own, deep down, in the darkness of the ocean, Kale and Faye swam. He smiled as he watched her flit around the sunken ship. She shone bright against the darkness of the wreckage. Her glowing hair reflected against her silver scales and made it easy for him to keep an eye on her.

He laughed at her antics. His sister was only a year younger than he was, but he felt much older. She was fearless and full of passion, never hesitating to pursue what she wanted. He admired her joy. For years his own heart had been too heavy to allow him to play.

Always uncannily quick to sense his feelings, Faye turned to him. "You're thinking of Adriana," she accused in a soft voice.

Adriana had been gone for years, but the sound of her name still sent ripples of pain through him. He nodded slowly. "Someone has to."

With a flick of her tail, Faye was at his side. "She has not been forgotten, brother."

"I wish I could believe that," he answered bitterly.

"It's just, the world of Merkin cannot mourn forever. We need to move on with our lives. What you're doing, it's not good."

"I am not mourning!" he snapped. "You only mourn the dead. She is alive, I can feel it. And I will never stop searching for her."

Faye flipped her tail in frustration. He couldn't say he blamed her. It had been years since everyone else had given up Adriana for dead. He couldn't even speak with his parents anymore about his quest for her.

He sighed deeply, and bubbles formed in the water. Faye giggled and poked at them. He envied her. Nothing could keep her spirit somber for long.

She flipped over and smacked him playfully with her tail. Suddenly she shivered, and spines rose up along her back. A mermaid's spines, ordinarily hidden in the smooth skin of her back, only rose for one of two reasons: fear or a premonition.

Kale glanced around uneasily but could neither see nor sense anything in the water, at least nothing that would elicit that reaction from her.

"What do you feel?" he asked in hushed tones. Only mermaids had premonitions; mermen did not. It was a defense honed by centuries of watching out for the safety of merchildren. As near as he could understand how it worked, they received strong feelings that told them when they needed to do something. The premonitions seemed to be uncontrollable. For most mermaids the sensation was so mild, it only pierced the subconscious. For a few, though—Faye included—the sensation was much stronger.

"We should go to the surface," she answered just as quietly.

He shuddered as though his scales had been rubbed the wrong way. He did not want to go. He had only been to the surface twice, both within days after Adriana's disappearance. It was an experience he had hoped never to repeat. He knew better, though, than to ignore one of Faye's premonitions.

He took a deep breath, and sucked in the water through his mouth. The gills on his throat flared widely for a moment as carbon dioxide was pushed out. "Let's go, then."

A flick of his tail sent him soaring upward through the water. A moment later Faye was back by his side. He whipped his tail back and forth and exhilarated at the feeling of the water rushing past his face and flowing over his body. Beside him, Faye kept up until they were flying through the water.

As they neared the surface, light began to stream downward, illuminating the darkness. As it grew brighter, Kale began to squint and his eyes burned. He slowed down, caution springing to mind. Beside him he could feel Faye's hesitation.

He reached out and took her hand and together they broke the surface with a gasp. Out of the water his cheeks stung and his eyes felt dry and scratchy. His lungs began to burn, and he eased his mouth back down into the water, chiding himself for forgetting to hold his breath.

He was about to ask Faye what they should do

next when he sensed a change in the motion of the water as it moved around him. Turning his head to the left, he spied a small boat.

It was tiny compared with the ones he had seen at the bottom of the ocean. It bobbed up and down on top of the water as it moved slowly toward them.

They've seen us! he thought. A moment later he realized it could not be so, because the two occupants of the boat seemed to be looking only at each other. He slipped below the surface of the water and pulled Faye with him. Together they moved closer to the boat, circling it warily. At last, the vessel stood still. A minute passed and nothing happened. Slowly they let their heads break the surface again.

He could hear the people speaking before he could see them. The sounds were strange to him and he could not glean any meaning from them. At last he could see the speakers clearly. There was a man leaning close to a woman. He had hair the color of the lava rock found in the deep parts of the ocean. He seemed to be speaking quite earnestly, but Kale couldn't understand the words.

He turned to look at the other occupant of the boat and felt his heart stop. *Adriana!* His soul knew her and cried out in such a mixture of joy and anguish as he had never felt.

He turned to Faye to tell her. The young mermaid was staring at the human male with rapt attention. Her eyes were wide, and she was drifting closer to the boat as though drawn to it. She reached out her hand to touch it.

"Faye!" he hissed.

She whirled, startled, and her spines raised. One of them hit the bottom of the boat, puncturing it. Moments later the man stood up in the boat and Kale and Faye both ducked beneath the water.

"Did you see?" he asked, gripping her arm.

"Yes, he was so beautiful."

"No, not him, her, it was Adriana!"

"What?"

"It was *Adriana*, in the boat."

"But that's impossible! Are you sure?" Faye asked, her face scrunching up in bewilderment.

"It was Adriana. I felt her."

"But . . . how?"

The boat began to move away, and he turned to follow it. He had spent years searching for her, and he wasn't about to lose her now. Faye swam beside him.

After a short distance the boat stopped again. *What are they doing?* Slowly, carefully, he lifted his head out of the water. Adriana and the man were both standing up. Suddenly, Adriana jumped overboard. The man jumped as well, but his foot got tangled in something that looked like seaweed in the bottom of the boat. He fell into the water, hitting his head with a dull thud against the bow.

Adriana was swimming on top of the water. Kale noted that she was moving and splashing with wasted motions, as though she were an infant. Her legs, swathed in heavy garments, flailed about uselessly, poor substitutes for the glorious tail she had once had. He moved to intercept her, but a motion he saw from the corner of his eye stopped him.

The man had sunk, unmoving, below the surface of the water. Faye reached out for him and before Kale could stop her, she clasped the human around the chest and hauled him back to the surface.

She coughed and sputtered as she struggled to keep her mouth below water and the man's above it. Kale moved to help her, but she waved him off.

"Make sure she makes it," she croaked.

For a moment he was torn between following Adriana or helping his sister. *At least Faye is not in any real danger as long as she takes a breath of water from time to time,* he told himself. With a flick of his tail he was off after Adriana.

She finally seemed to find her own rhythm. It was awkward looking, but it seemed to be working. He swam just behind and below her, keeping a watchful eye.

All the time, his thoughts were racing. He didn't know which was harder to believe: that he had finally found her, or that she had been turned into a human. He needed to make contact with her, and find a way to turn her back into a mermaid.

She faltered in the water and he surged forward, ready to buoy her up if she needed it. She picked up her own rhythm, though, and pressed on.

The closer they came to shore, the more

relieved he became regarding her safety and the greater he worried about his own. She came to a stop and he waited. He watched her as she treaded the water above him. The pull of the ocean toward the shore had grown strong, and he had to start putting energy into keeping himself from letting it carry him forward.

She started swimming again, and moments later a wave picked her up and carried her to dry land. He lifted his head out of the water, watching as she lay on the sand, coughing. Slowly she stood to her feet, and he breathed a sigh of relief. She didn't seem to be hurt.

She began shouting and then turned and ran up the beach. She was probably looking for the man. He turned and scanned the water for Faye. She was out past the waves, still supporting the human. He moved to help her.

"We have to get him up onto the land without her seeing us."

"Why? If it truly is Adriana, why should it matter if she sees us?" Faye gasped, her voice sounding unnaturally loud and piercing to him as she spoke into the air.

"She has been turned into a human. Who knows if she has any memory of who she is? I need time to think how best to approach her."

"Kale, you worry too much," Faye informed him.

They watched as Adriana raced down the beach in the other direction, still shouting. She turned again and began to walk, half stumbling back up the beach again.

"All right, now," Kale said.

"How will we get him up on the sand?"

"Let a wave carry him in."

She shook her head fiercely. "If he remains unconscious with his head in the water, he'll die."

"We can't risk getting closer to the shore."

"I didn't bring him this far to let him drown now. We're awake, so we have a better chance of helping him get to the land without hurting ourselves than he has of getting there carried by the tides."

Kale knew she was right. They had to keep the human's head above the water. "I have an idea. When I say so, start swimming, on top of the water. We want the waves to lift us up on the sand. Remember to take a deep breath and hold it."

She nodded, eyes wide.

He turned and studied the waves. A large one was rolling toward them. "Ready. Now!"

He took a deep breath, turned, and grabbed hold of the man. The wave caught the three of them and lifted them up onto the sand. Kale lay for a moment, stunned. Involuntarily, he gasped. As the air rushed into his lungs he began to suffocate. He flipped over on his stomach, beating at the sand with his tail. He grabbed fistfuls of wet sand and began dragging his body back to the water. He started to grow faint. His lungs were burning, and his vision swam. Just when he thought he was going to collapse, a wave splashed up higher than the others and flooded his mouth with water. He breathed in with a great gasp and used the last of his strength to propel his body into the water, where he drifted for a moment gathering his strength.

He heard a sound beside him and turned to see Faye doing the same thing. "Will he live?" he asked.

"I don't know. I think so," she answered.

He nodded. "Time for us to go." He dragged himself a few more feet into the water before he could get his tail clear. Then he shot forward several yards and turned when he felt himself a safe distance from the sand.

Faye was still at the edge of the water, and he grew alarmed. Did she not have the strength to drag herself into the water? She stirred then, and he could not believe his eyes. She was dragging herself back to the man's side!

She bent low over him, and he watched in disbelief as she kissed the still figure. Then she jerked her head up as though startled and quickly pulled herself back to the water. Within moments she had cleared the sand. She glided up to him with a guilty look on her face. "He's alive," she confirmed.

"Did he see you?"

She dropped her eyes. "Yes," she whispered.

He felt himself grow cold inside. "Then we must go, quickly."

"I don't think he saw my tail."

"We can't take that risk. We must go now and we shall not speak of this to anyone."

As they dove beneath the waves, Kale was afraid to think about what they had just done. They didn't speak until they had reached the sunken ship Faye had been exploring earlier.

Faye was the first to break the silence. "What could have turned Adriana into a human?"

Kale grimaced. "I have my suspicions."

She nodded slowly. "It would have to be, wouldn't it? There's no other way this could have happened."

"None that I know of."

"So, can she be changed back?"

"I wish I knew," he told her, his heart heavy with doubt. Just as big a problem as changing her back would be telling her what she really was. Having watched her swim, he was convinced she could have no memory of who she really was. Then, provided he could convince her of the truth and find a way to change her back, would she even want to return?

"Who do you think he was?"

Startled, he looked at Faye. "What?"

"The man, who do you think he was?"

Kale shook his head. "I have no idea."

She sighed heavily. "He was so beautiful."

Kale threw her a sharp glance. The tone in her voice made him nervous. "Best to forget about him, Faye. Merkin and humans are not meant to interact. What happened today was an accident, and we must try and forget it even happened."

He recognized the fire that flashed in her eyes. He had seen it there before and it had always meant trouble. He was going to have to keep an eye on his little sister.

Kale was worried. Faye had disappeared after dinner, and now with the morning it was apparent that she had never returned home. He never should have let her out of his sight, not with what she had said about the human and the look of defiance she had given him.

There is but one person who could have changed Adriana into a human, he thought. Faye knew that as well, and he feared that she might have done something foolish in her desire to see the human male again. There was only one way to find out.

He had to visit the Sea Witch.

The Sea Witch lived outside the borders of the world of mer-kin, and though all knew how to reach her caves, all merkin were forbidden to have any contact with her. Violation of that law could result in banishment for the merkin foolish enough to speak with her. Years before she had ruled over the kingdom of the dryads and had waged war against the merkin. Dryads were distant cousins to merkin; indeed, the two were often mistaken for one another by humans. Instead of tales, though, the dryads had bodies that more closely resembled sea serpents, long and slender. The Witch had risen to power among the dryads and eventually claimed that throne, killing many of her own kind in the process. During the great war that ensued, Kale and Adriana's ancestors had been instrumental in defeating the Witch and sending her into exile.

The Witch couldn't be killed—at least, that was the legend. The best their forefathers had been able to do was help her own people depose her. She lived in exile from her kind. No one knew how strong her magic was or from where it came.

Since he had seen Adriana as a human there had been little doubt in his mind as to how she had gotten that way. The Sea Witch, an ancient, evil crone, was the only one capable of performing that kind of magic.

He shuddered as he thought about all the stories he had heard as a young merchild. Some said that the reason no one had been able to kill the Witch was because she was immortal and that she was actually thousands of years old and had been partly responsible for the destruction of ancient islands and civilizations. A cousin of one of his friends had wandered too near the Sea Witch's caves, and she had cursed him so that he died excruciatingly, his scales peeling off slowly and his internal organs shifting about on their own. They said, in the end, that he had coughed up his own heart.

Mother and Father will kill me if they hear I've come here, risking my life, breaking the law, disgracing my family . . . if the Witch doesn't kill me first. . . .

As he neared the sea caves he felt a change in the water; there was a chill that wasn't present elsewhere. All he could think about was the boy choking on his own heart. He pressed on, though everything in him was screaming to turn back.

At the entrance to the largest cave he stopped. "Hello?" he called.

"Come in," a silky voice whispered.

He floated in slowly, eyes adjusting to a dark that was greater than any he had ever known. The blackness was caused by more than the depth of the sea or a lack of light; it was a darkness that seemed to emanate from the very walls of the cave. At last he came into a sort of room and saw her.

The Witch was hideous in appearance. Her upper body was like a mermaid's, only twisted and disfigured. The rest of her body was that of a sea serpent. Coils lay draped over the bare stone and disappeared into the darkness, so that he had no idea of her true length. Hair like seaweed seemed to have a life of its own as it hung around her. The only thing of beauty was a string of pearls she wore around her neck. Each pearl was huge and dark in color, glowing with a luster all its own.

The only light in the room came from a cage at one end, where a host of iridescent fish swam, trapped and helpless. He gulped, hoping that she wasn't using the fish for anything other than a light source. *I heard she eats her own kind*, the thought popped into his head. Aside from them, the room was empty and barren. He looked back at her and realized the blackness he had earlier thought had been coming from the very walls of the cave were instead coming from her, like ink being sprayed by an octopus; her very skin seemed to give off some sort of black oil. *Dark as her soul . . .*

"What do you seek of the Sea Witch?" she hissed, her forked tongue flicking out between her fangs.

Faced with her, he knew that he had been foolish to think that she would give him answers, foolish to think that he could come here demanding things from her and even manage to escape with his life. Even if he did manage to ask her about Adriana and Faye, she would never tell him—there was no gain in it for her. No, *I'll just have to be clever. There must be some other way to find out if she changed them and how she did it.*

Suddenly he was speaking, and he was astonished at the words coming out of his mouth. "I wish to be human."

She cackled, and the sound sent chills up his spine. "And why would a prince of the merkin want that?"

He gasped. "You know who I am."

She laughed, and the sound frightened him more than any he had ever heard. "Of course I know. I am, after all, *me*." She paused just long enough to let that sink in and to let him wonder what else she might know. "You are Kale, and you are one of the royal princes of the merkin, descended from Glandria, are you not?"

He refused to answer her, though she was right.

She smiled coyly. "No need to answer, for I know the truth. Now tell me, Kale of the merkin, why do you want to be human?"

"I have fallen in love with a human," he blurted.

"Yes, there seems to be a lot of that going around," she said with amusement.

Faye had been to see her, just as he'd feared. *Faye, what have you done?* The only way he could help her now, and speak with Adriana, was to follow. He took a deep breath. "Can you change me?"

"Well, it isn't that easy, my young one. Nothing comes without a price. You say you would do this for love?"

He nodded, not trusting himself to speak.

"And the young lady, does she love you?"

"I do not know, I hope so," he answered truthfully.

"Loving is always a risk, you know," she told him in a conversational tone. "You open up to someone and you risk rejection and ridicule. That's the risk everyone who loves takes. You, though, you seem to be willing to risk a bit more. You are willing to risk leaving your home and your family to travel to a strange world where you might have to live out your days alone. Is that true?"

He nodded, his anxiety increasing with every word she spoke.

"My, my, that certainly is a lot to risk," she said as she circled him slowly. "Well, if you are willing to risk that much, then surely you will be willing to risk just a little bit more."

"What?" he whispered.

She was behind him now and she put her lips close to his ear. Her tongue flicked out, tickling him. "Your life."

"No!" he shouted, spinning around.

She pressed her finger against his lips. "Ssshh. Wait until you hear the deal."

"I will turn you into a human. You will then have seven days to convince the young lady to fall in love with you. By sunset on the seventh day, she must agree to marry you. If she does, you will then live out your life with her, happily ever after."

"And if she doesn't?"

"Then you will die and your soul will die with you."

He reeled back, aghast. Merkin believed that the soul lived on even after the body had died and that it went to a better place. They also believed that the souls of the dead watched out for their living descendants. *Could the Witch actually kill the soul as well as the body?* Looking into her eyes, he had no choice but to believe it, for he could see no soul within her.

"No, the price is too high." He shook his head, hoping the movement would shake him free of the hypnotic spell her voice was weaving around him.

"Suit yourself," the Witch said, and started to slither away. She glanced back over her shoulder. "You must not love her very much, though, if you're not willing to take the risk. Maybe the women of your species have all the courage. A young mermaid was in here just this morning, and *she* did not think the price too high."

Faye! She would be dead within a week if she could not win the love of the man she had saved. Kale had to help her, to save her. He wouldn't be able to help her down here, though. "I . . . accept the risk."

The Witch slithered back toward him, an evil smile dancing across her face. "Let us get started, then."

He allowed her to lead him into the darkest recesses of the cave. At her bidding, he sat in the center of a huge clamshell. She slithered around him and whispered words that he could not understand. She finally stopped before him, and he noticed the pearls around her neck were glowing. They grew brighter by the moment, and the Witch began rubbing the strand between her thumb and forefinger.

"Will I look like them?" he asked, hating the tremor in his voice.

"Yes."

"What about their garments?"

"I can provide you with something, if you wish, if you'll answer a question."

"Wh—what?"

"Your lady—has she seen you, heard your voice?"

"No."

"Have you heard hers?"

"No," he replied, panicking now. "Will I be able to understand her, and will she understand me?"

"Yes," the Witch said with a casual wave of her hand. "So, how will you know her?"

"I have seen her."

"Ah. Is she beautiful?"

"Very beautiful."

"Do you know where to find her or what name she is called by?"

"No, I do not," he said, realizing for the first time that she might not even go by the name Adriana.

"So, the only way you can find her is by *seeing* her?"

"Yes."

The Witch cackled with satisfaction. "Good luck in finding her, then . . . without your *eyes!*"

Kale opened his mouth to ask what she meant, but blinding pain ripped through him and only a scream came out. His body felt as though it were being split in two. His vision began to fade, and the last things he saw before everything went black were the glowing pearls.

"You didn't think it would be that easy, did you?" Her voice pierced the haze of his pain. "You didn't think I would extract some price for my services? You might be willing to gamble everything, but I am not."

"How am I to find her?" he shouted, raising his hands before him and groping for the wall.

"That is your problem, not mine," she said, the voice fading as though she were moving away from him.

"What could you possibly gain from my death?"

"Let's just say that the suffering of your kind is the prize I am seeking. I'm sure the death of one of their princes would bring quite a lot of suffering. Speaking of which, you have about five minutes before the transformation is complete and you can no longer breathe water.

"If I were you, I'd start swimming."

"Help me!" he shouted.

There was no answer. The Sea Witch was gone.

His lungs were starting to ache, and it was getting harder to breathe. He tried to push off from the clamshell, but his disintegrating tail failed him. Desperately he flailed out with his arms as he had seen Adriana do when she was swimming for the shore.

He could feel himself moving forward through the water, but at an agonizingly slow rate. He bumped into the wall and, disoriented, he felt for the passage through which he had come. At last he found it and made his way back out of the cave.

He swam as fast as he could, heading for the surface, and eventually the water grew warmer around him, the cold of the Witch's lair fading behind him. His body was still changing, he could feel it, and the pain was unbearable. He was having a harder time with each breath he tried to draw, and desperation lent him strength. He kicked and splashed, swimming as fast as he could.

He began to choke and at the same time he could feel his tail split completely. He gave a mighty kick first with one half and then the other—*no, my legs!* he corrected himself—and his head broke the surface of the water.

He gasped, sucking in the air, drinking it as he had once breathed the water. He treaded the water for a moment, taking deep breaths and coughing up water. His new legs suddenly seemed heavier. He reached down to touch them with his hand. There seemed to be some covering over them. The Witch had at least given him some clothing.

At last his breathing evened out. He needed to make it to the shore, though he wasn't sure how much longer he could swim. Without his eyes he would have to find another way to locate the land. If he set off in the wrong direction he wouldn't discover the mistake in time to save himself.

He heard the sound of the waves crashing on the beach. On his body he still felt the play of the water. The gentle waves moved in one direction while the undertow pulled in the opposite direction. He turned and began to swim with the tide.

❖ Chapter Six ❖

She walked down the aisle, staring at her groom as he stood beside Father Gregory. He smiled at her, and the gesture sent shivers up her spine. She prayed that God would have mercy and strike her dead before she reached them.

"James!" she shouted as loud as she could.

When there was no reply, Pearl turned and tried to run down the beach. Her wet skirt slowed her, and she fell to her knees several times. She kept struggling back up, though. She reached the end of the beach and turned around, running back the other way. Nothing.

She headed back up the beach more slowly, inspecting the sand for footprints as well. Maybe, just maybe, he had reached the beach first and went to get help. She clung to the slender thread of hope, though in her heart she didn't believe it. He would not have left with her still in the water.

The only sets of footprints she found farther up the beach were hers and the ones they had left earlier when they'd arrived. She turned back and scanned the length of the beach once more.

There! There was something dark on the sand.

She picked up her skirt and ran, stumbling toward it. When she got closer she saw that it was James, lying in a crumpled heap on the sand.

She fell on her knees beside him, sobbing. Slowly, he straightened up and looked at her wide-eyed.

"You saved me."

"No," she said, shaking her head.

"You did, I saw you," he insisted.

Confusion filled her. "James, I—I thought I'd lost you."

"My foot got tangled in the rope, and I hit my head on the bow of the boat. I woke up here with you leaning over me. You saved me."

"I didn't. I just found you, here on the beach. Maybe the tide carried you in."

He shook his head groggily. "No, it was you. You bent down and kissed me and then . . . you went away."

"James, I didn't save you and I didn't kiss you."

"Well, somebody did and she had your hair and your beautiful skin. So, if it wasn't you, who was it?"

"I don't know," she said, rocking back on her heels and preparing to stand.

He grabbed her hand, and his voice dropped low. It was commanding, insistent. "I shall marry the girl who saved me."

She stared into his eyes for a long moment with her heart in her throat. He thought it was she. *And what of it?* He had been dreaming; no one else had been on the beach but her. The tide must have washed him up.

But what if it didn't? her mind demanded. Then James would be marrying the wrong woman. *And who has more right to marry him than me?* She flushed at her own arrogance.

Tears fell from her eyes and landed on his cheek. "Then you shall not be marrying me."

Pearl sat on her bed with her knees tucked under her chin. For all the years they had known each other, she and James had never parted on uneasy terms. He refused to believe that she hadn't saved him from drowning. It would have been so easy to lie to him, but she had never lied to him about anything before and she wasn't about to start. She owed him the truth even if he wouldn't accept it.

When she had come home her parents had taken one look at her bedraggled form and wisely refrained from asking questions. Despite her anxiety over James, she was also more than a little amazed that she had survived her swim in the ocean.

"The voice was wrong," she whispered. And if the voice was wrong about that, it could be wrong about other things. Maybe she was somebody, somebody special.

Long after the cottage had grown dark and quiet, she finally lay down and closed her eyes. She fell asleep, and the dreams came.

The boat was behind her, and she was swimming for the shore. She was afraid she wouldn't make it. If you go in the water, you will die, *the voice in her head whispered.* But the rush of water against her skin felt good. She glanced back but did not see James. Behind her, though, just beneath the surface of the water, there was a shadow. The shadow's eyes stared at her. They always stare.

The eyes beckoned her down into the depths, below the surface, into the darkness. She followed, swimming, laughing. She felt so alive.

The shadow disappeared, and the world grew dark as night. The water was cold. It hurt her skin, it was so cold. It wasn't as cold as the laughter, though—that seemed to come from everywhere. The darkness threatened to overwhelm her, and she whimpered.

There was a light shining in the darkness, and she was drawn to it. In the light there were pearls, beautiful and large. She reached out and took one of them and hid it away.

Then came the voice—the hard one, not the soft one. It floated on the water. "Never return. . . . If you go into the ocean you will die along with everyone you love. . . . You are nothing, nobody. . . . No one will miss you. . . ." There were other words, but she couldn't hear them.

"I won't die," she yelled. "I won't die."

She woke up whispering, "I won't die."

The nightmares faded back into the darkness, and she was left alone in the cold light of morning. She had something, though, the barest shred of a memory, but it was more than she had ever had and she clung to it as a child clings to her mother's skirt.

The night that Finneas had pulled her out of the ocean, the water had been cold.

The day passed in a blur of misery. She spent most of the afternoon cleaning and preserving fish that her father had caught that morning. At dinner everyone ate in a silence that she was grateful for. Afterward she excused herself and headed for the beach.

She both desired and dreaded to see James and wasn't at all sure which emotion was stronger. It was not his day to be at the beach, but a part of her hoped he would be there, waiting for her.

As she crested the hill she had to shield her eyes against the rays of the sun as it approached the horizon. Someone was sitting on the beach facing the ocean. *Sitting in our spot.* With the sun in her eyes she couldn't tell who it was, but was sure it must be James.

She was within ten feet of the man before she realized that he was a stranger. Startled, she stopped. The man was naked from the waist up and was cradling his head in his hands. His shoulders were broad and well-muscled. His large hands looked powerful, whereas the long, slender fingers added an air of grace to them. His legs, clad in simple pants, seemed impossibly long and were stretched out on the sand. He had pale hair, nearly silver like hers. His skin was also deathly white with patches of red where the sun of the day had burned him.

Suddenly the man lifted his head, and she took a step back. He cocked his head as though listening, and sniffed the air as an animal would. "Adriana?" he asked softly.

"I'm sorry, sir, you are mistaken," she informed him.

A smile burst over his face, and she jumped back as he scrambled to his feet like a newborn colt. "Adriana! It *is* you!"

"I'm sorry, sir, I do not know this Adriana of whom you speak. I am Pearl."

"Pearl. . . ," he said slowly, as though he were tasting the word in his mouth.

His presence here on her beach and in such a state of undress unnerved her and she backed up, ready to flee. It was then that he finally looked at her.

She gasped and stopped in her tracks. *His eyes!* They were the dark eyes from her dreams. The eyes of the shadow that always stood behind James. "You, who are you?" she asked, feeling dazed.

"I am Kale, and I have been searching for you for a very long time."

"Searching for Adriana, you mean."

"Searching for *you*, no matter what name you are called by here."

She felt dizzy, as though she were standing on the edge of a precipice. It was then that she noticed the eerie fixation of his eyes, their unblinking stare. "Your eyes?" she asked.

He raised his hand to them. "A recent development seems to have rendered me blind."

"Then how did you know it was me?"

"Your scent, the sound of your voice, your spirit— all these things made you known to me."

She backed up a bit. "You are frightening me, sir."

"I guess I must be, at that. I am sorry. I'm a bit frightened myself."

"Are you ill?"

"Not exactly, though it would be safe to say that I am not myself today."

His comments were so cryptic that for a moment, she believed he might be insane. His state of undress did nothing to convince her otherwise. Still, she could not turn from him, from the owner of the eyes that she saw every night in her dreams.

"Why do you believe that I am this woman you are seeking?"

He sighed heavily. "I saw you yesterday and recognized you."

"But your eyes . . ."

"I told you, the blindness is a recent complication, *very* recent."

"Why did you not make yourself known to me yesterday?" she asked suspiciously.

"Believe me, I wanted to, but circumstances prevented it. Also, it seemed that you and the young man wished to be alone."

She felt her blood run cold. He had seen her with James! She took a step back. Was he some enemy of James's, or someone who wanted to hurt his reputation, or hers?

"You saw us?"

He nodded. "Is he all right?"

"Yes." He had seen the accident, then. She looked

again at his eyes. They were such a deep color. She had thought that they were black, but as she looked closer she saw that they were a dark shade of blue, the most intense eyes she had ever seen. *Except for the shadow.* Something from her dream suddenly came back to her. She was swimming away from the boat and she saw the shadow in the water beneath her, the eyes fixed upon her.

"You! You were in the water with me yesterday," she accused.

He suddenly looked very agitated. "Yes, I was," he admitted. "Did you see me?"

"Only your eyes," she admitted.

He seemed to relax at that. "I followed you to make sure you made it safely to the land."

She stared at his silver hair, and a sickening feeling twisted her stomach. "Was there someone else with you?" she asked in hushed tones.

He nodded. "My sister, Faye."

"She saved James," Pearl said more to herself than to him.

"That is true," he affirmed.

She felt as though her world were crashing down around her. "Where is she now?"

"I don't know," he admitted. "I think she went off in search of him this morning."

Her legs gave way, and she sank slowly to a seat on the sand. *James is going to marry her!* She felt as though she couldn't breathe, and within moments tears were coursing down her cheeks. Awkwardly he dropped back down to the sand. At last the wave passed and she glanced at Kale.

"You really care about him, don't you?" he asked.

"It's . . . complicated," she said.

"Why is it complicated? Either you love him or not."

"It's just not that easy."

"Why?"

"He's my best friend and my prince," she answered, not sure why she wanted to suddenly pour her heart out to this stranger. *He doesn't feel like a stranger, though. There's something so familiar about him, like I've known him all my life.* Warning bells were going off in her head. She shouldn't be speaking with him, a strange man alone on the beach. And she definitely shouldn't be telling him anything about her relationship with James.

"But you love him?" he pressed, his voice wistful sounding.

She answered despite herself. "I don't know. I think I have feelings for him. I *do* have feelings for him, I just don't know if I love him."

"Then you don't," he said confidently. "If you have to question whether you're in love, then you're not."

She shuddered. "It would just be so easy to be in love with him. It would solve so many problems." She sighed, frustrated. "But it would create so many more. He's a prince and I am nothing."

"That is a lie!"

Startled, she stared at him. "What do you mean?"

"You are not nothing, and anyone who said you are is *lying*."

"How—how do you know that?"

He smiled gently. "I told you, I have been searching for you for years."

She looked at his earnest face, pale skin, and silver hair and believed him. Her heart began to pound. "Do you know where I come from? Who my real parents are?"

"Yes."

"Are they alive?" she asked, fighting to speak around the lump in her throat.

"Yes. And they will be very happy to find that you are too. They searched for you for years after you disappeared, until they finally resigned themselves to believing that you were dead."

"They thought I was killed in the storm?"

A look of puzzlement flitted across his face for only a moment. "They weren't sure what happened to you."

"And you. You say you kept searching for me?"

"Yes."

"You've traveled far?" she asked.

He laughed shortly. "Farther than you know."

His words held the ring of truth. There was more than that, though. Something about him drew her to him. As if sensing her thoughts, he reached out his hand to her.

She touched his hand with her own and he clasped it in his, lowering them to rest on the sand. She stared at her pale fingers wrapped in his. *We must have come from the same place,* she thought with growing excitement. "Are you my brother?"

"No, I'm not. We are not related."

"Good," she answered before she could stop herself. She felt a blush rising to her cheeks and was grateful that he couldn't see it.

He was rubbing the back of her hand with his thumb, and her skin tingled where his touched hers. *James did the same thing to my hand two days ago and it felt good, exciting, but nothing like this. . . . Something about him feels so right, even though I don't know him.*

She was suddenly nervous; the silence around them felt like the air did when a storm approached from across the sea. She spoke just to calm herself. "You've been searching how long?"

"Thirteen years."

"How did you know it was me if you haven't seen me in so long?"

"How does the whale know when to swim to warmer waters for winter? How do the fish know when a predator is near? How do you know when love is real? You just know."

He was close, so close that she could feel the warmth radiating from his body. She felt herself flush again, and tiny chills raced up and down her spine. "You speak of love so intimately. Have you known it yourself?"

"I have," he whispered.

Disappointment flooded her. He was in love with someone. She should not sit so close to him, or let him hold her hand, or think the thoughts she was thinking. "Who . . . who are you in love with?" she asked.

"You."

"Me!" she gasped.

His voice dropped down to the barest of whispers. "Have you ever known that something was going to happen just before it did, or acted without knowing quite why?"

She remembered the boy she had saved from the runaway cart. She had known something was wrong a moment before she realized what it was. That was why she had been able to grab him in time. *Nor is that the first time something like that has happened. But I have never told anyone.*

"Yes."

"Then I am sure your instincts tell you what I'm going to do next."

She held her breath as he slid his hand up her arm and along her neck until he was cupping her chin. He bent forward and kissed her, his lips soft against hers. She could taste the ocean on him as his kiss turned from the gentleness of lapping waves to the passion of a storm. As he wrapped both his arms around her she knew that she was drowning in his embrace.

The last ray of the setting sun was shining upon his face when they parted. She touched his cheek wonderingly. "Who are you?"

"I am Kale. I am your betrothed."

"My what?" she gasped.

Before he could answer, she heard her father's flute, the notes drifting to her on the air, calling her home. She stood up quickly, confused and suddenly upset. "I have to go." She turned and headed away at a run before he could gain his feet.

"Adriana!" he shouted after her.

She kept running, confusion ripping at her.

"Adriana!" he called again. Just as she passed behind the hill she heard him cry out, "Pearl!"

She had no idea what had just happened, but she knew she had to get home. She needed time to think. When the cottage came into sight she saw a few horses in front of it. She slowed to a walk, breathless. Father must have visitors. She smoothed her dress and checked her hair. She brushed away her tears and entered the cabin.

Three men in fine garments stood talking with her parents. Both Mary and Finneas looked agitated. Finneas glanced over at her, and his face broke out in a smile of relief.

"Ah, here she is. My lord, may I introduce my daughter, Pearl. Pearl, this is Robert, marquis of Novan, son of the duke of Novan."

She curtsied low, ducking her eyes. She jumped when he picked up her hand and kissed the back of her fingers. "My lady, it is an honor to meet you at last."

She gazed first from him to Finneas. Both men were smiling. Mary, too, was smiling, though Pearl could tell that she had been crying.

Finally she turned back to Robert. "My lord, to what do we owe the honor of your visit?"

His smile grew broader. "Well, I've actually come to speak with your father on a matter of great importance. As your father, it is his privilege to tell you."

"Tell me what?" she asked, turning toward Finneas. Tears were gleaming in his eyes too.

"You tell her, my lord."

"Finneas, given our new relationship, I believe it would be proper for you to address me as Robert."

"What relationship?" she asked, wishing someone would tell her what was going on.

Robert smiled and took a step closer to her. He bent down and peered into her eyes. "My dear Pearl, I am your betrothed."

❖ Chapter Seven ❖

Faye sat upon the sand and tried to scream. The pain was more than she could bear. Her tail had been ripped in half and forced into the shape of two human legs. Bone and muscle and nerves had been twisted, torn, and re-formed into something new and totally strange to her. She screamed and screamed, but no sound came out. Her voice had been sacrificed to the Sea Witch.

She fell onto her back and could feel the sand burrowing into the pores of her flesh. The sun beat down upon her, and pain seared through her. Her skin felt as though it were drying out, her eyes burned, and her lungs heaved while trying to breathe the air. Surely she must die; merkin could not survive outside of the sea, and it had been folly to believe that she could.

She would have rolled into the ocean but she didn't have the strength. *So, I am to die here. Away from my family, my people, my home. I was a fool.*

She managed to flip onto her side. More pain sliced through her body, and she whimpered. The gravity of what she had done shot through her. She had one week to find the man she loved and win his love. If she failed, she would die. If she succeeded, she would live, but in the state she now found herself. *Maybe it is better to die quickly than spend a lifetime in agony.*

She rolled over onto her stomach and began to cough. Seawater poured out of her mouth and seeped into the sand. At long last her chest stopped heaving. Suddenly the hair on the back of her neck stood on end.

"Pearl? Are you all right?"

She turned her head and saw *him*. Her heart began to sing. "Sorry, I—I thought you were someone else." She opened her mouth to speak, to tell him of her love, but no sound came out. Frustrated, she shook her head.

He came closer to her. "Do you need help?"

She nodded fiercely. He looked at her wide-eyed before hastily shrugging out of his outer garment. He handed it to her and then averted his eyes.

She felt heat rising in her cheeks as she took the garment from him. She had watched him remove his arms from part of it and she tried to emulate that. At last she had it wrapped around herself.

He still stood, face turned away, and she had no voice to tell him he could turn back. She picked up a handful of sand and threw it at his leg.

He whipped his head back around to look at her, and a smile broke out on his face. He crouched down beside her. "That's better. So, where are you from?"

She twisted and pointed out to the ocean, marveling

at how the pain in her limbs seemed to have lessened since he appeared.

"From far away, then." He scanned the horizon. "You must have been shipwrecked. How long have you been here?"

She looked up at him, helpless to answer. *He is so beautiful!* His hair was dark, like the depths of the ocean. His eyes were brilliant blue, like the surface of the water. She ached to touch him, to smooth his hair back from his face and to tell him he was everything to her. *Hear me, know my thoughts if not my words!* He stared back at her, and slowly his eyes widened. He crouched down and touched her hair with his hand. "You, you were the one who saved me?" he asked.

She nodded eagerly, her eyes beginning to sting. *Did he hear me or is he just remembering? It doesn't really matter so long as he knows.*

"You were the one who pulled me from the sea?"

She nodded again.

"And you were the one who—"

She leaned forward and kissed him. When she pulled back there was a light dancing in his eyes.

"Yes, you were the one," he whispered.

The castle was enormous, and Faye felt small within its shadow.

At the beach the young man who introduced himself as James had left her briefly and returned with some simple garments more appropriate for her to wear. It had been a struggle, but she had managed to get into them. Walking had proven even more difficult, and James had finally picked her up and carried her.

The building would have frightened her had it not been for James's arms around her. Their entrance seemed to generate a great deal of excitement. People were running around everywhere, some whispering, others shouting.

"This is my father's castle," James explained. "He is the king and I am the prince."

She smiled at him encouragingly. *Like my brother. At least that would please my parents,* she thought, laughing.

"It's not every day they see me walk in carrying a gorgeous woman." He laughed.

An older man approached them. "Highness, may I be of assistance?"

"Yes, Peter. This is the young woman who saved my life. She's the survivor of a shipwreck. Can you see that she is taken care of?"

Peter glanced at her, taking in her disheveled appearance. He looked like a kind man, and Faye smiled at him. The ghost of a smile touched his lips in return. "I'll see to it that she is presentable by dinnertime."

"Sooner, if you can. She and I have a lot to discuss. She seems to have sprained her ankles and she's lost her voice."

"Then you'll be doing all the talking and she'll be

doing all the listening. That sounds familiar," Peter remarked dryly.

James laughed. "I listen to you."

Peter snapped his fingers, and a large woman with a merry face scurried forward. "Sarah, help me get the lady to her room."

James gently set Faye down on her feet. She began to sway, but Peter and Sarah caught her. They urged her to drape her arms around their shoulders and walk between them. She did as she was bid.

Each step was less painful than the one before it, and by the time they reached the end of the room she wasn't wobbling half so much. Once they got her upstairs and into a room, they lowered her down onto a piece of furniture that seemed made for sitting upon.

She sighed in relief and rubbed her feet.

"My lady, I will be leaving you in Sarah's care. She can see to anything you require," Peter said.

She nodded that she understood. He bowed deeply and left the room.

Sarah gazed cheerfully at her. "Well, my lady, let's get you cleaned up, shall we?"

Before she knew what was happening, she had been dumped into a large tub of hot water. She laughed silently. *Looks like I'm back in the water again!* The water was different from what she was used to, though. It felt different on her skin and it smelled and tasted different as well.

She could tell that Sarah was laughing at her, but

she didn't care, it just made her laugh harder. By the time she made it out of the bathtub she was exhausted.

Next, Sarah tried to dress her in yards and yards of fabric. They both had the giggles by the time it was done. At last Sarah stood back. "Well, you're looking like a lady now, and a beautiful one at that," she asserted.

Faye blushed, pleased by the compliment.

"Now, let's not keep the prince waiting any longer," Sarah gushed. She led Faye from the room and downstairs to the main floor. Off the great hall was a chamber with a roaring fire and several chairs and couches.

Her heart skipped a beat as she recognized James pacing before the fire. He turned to see her, and a huge smile wreathed his face. He strode forward and clasped her hands. "You look radiant." He turned to Sarah, "Thank you, Mrs. Goodman. I appreciate your efforts."

It was Sarah's turn to blush as she curtsied deeply. She excused herself and hurried out, leaving them alone.

James led her to a seat and she accepted it gratefully. Her legs seemed to be getting stronger by the minute, but they were still sore and a little weak.

"I want to know everything about you," he told her, sitting beside her. "Is your voice any better?"

She tried to speak even though she knew she would not be able to. No sound came out, and she shook her head.

"It's no matter. I've had an idea," he told her. His enthusiasm was contagious, and she couldn't help but smile.

"I have parchment, a quill, and some ink. You can draw the answers."

He showed her a large, flat piece of paper. He pulled an ornately carved wooden table over in front of her and placed the parchment on top of it. He also put down a bottle of dark liquid that made her think of the ink an octopus would spit at an enemy. Mer-kin had learned to use that ink to make markings upon rocks and shells. Lastly he handed her a slender instrument topped with a feather. She stared at it, puzzled.

With a laugh, he took it back from her. "Let me show you. You dip the pen in the ink, and draw upon the parchment like so."

She watched as he demonstrated. At last she grasped the pen and gave it a try, delighted as dark lines sprang to life on the parchment. The markings looked clearer and they required less effort than the manner of writing they had at home.

"Excellent!" he encouraged her. "Now, where do you come from?"

She thought for a moment and then drew the waves on top of the ocean. He studied it for a moment with a puzzled frown.

"Ah! Your people are seafaring, like the Norse."

She wanted to tell him that she came from under the ocean, that she dwelt among the fish and other sea creatures. She bit her lip, debating whether to try to tell him. She looked into his eyes and believed in her heart of hearts that he would accept what she had to say.

Still, it would be better to wait, a voice told her. Better to let him truly know her before she burdened him with that story. She sighed.

"I have a friend who looks a lot like you," he commented as he touched her hair. "She was found at sea when she was a child. Her name is Pearl. I wonder if your people are hers?"

Faye smiled weakly and shrugged her shoulders. She would have to tell him about Adriana eventually, but was less sure how to go about that than she was about how to tell him about her own ancestry.

"What is your name?" he asked, breaking into her thoughts.

She was at a loss as to what to draw and just looked at him helplessly. He seemed to sense her difficulty and hurried to ask, "What does it sound like?"

She didn't need pen and parchment for that one. She touched his face.

"Face?" he asked, looking startled. "It sounds like 'face'?"

She nodded, then held her hands at shoulders' width from each other and then brought them slowly together.

"It's shorter than face, it sounds like only part of face?"

She nodded eagerly.

"Ffffaa—"

She nodded again.

"Faye?"

She clapped her hands together and smiled.

"Faye," he said again, beaming. "Well, that was simple. I am James, prince of Aster."

She laughed silently. Her mother would be so pleased to know that she had fallen in love with a prince. In her world, her family was also royalty. That was why Kale and Adriana had been betrothed since birth.

Her smile faded as she thought of home and her family. She looked down at the skirt wrapped around her legs. *Human legs.* Sorrow weighed heavily upon her. Would she ever see her brother and parents again? She had left behind so much, was it worth it?

James put a hand under her chin and lifted her eyes to meet his. As she stared into their depths, she knew that it was.

"Do you miss your home?" he asked.

She smiled, wondering if her thoughts had been that transparent. She nodded slightly.

"Can I help you get back there?" he asked, his face anxious.

She shook her head and a smile crept over his face.

"Then I'm just going to have to make sure you're happy here," he said.

He slid his hand from under her chin to touch her cheek and slowly bent toward her. Her breath caught in her throat, and her heart started to flutter excitedly in her chest.

When his lips met hers they were soft and warm and held a promise that she scarcely dared believe. She lost herself in his kiss and knew that she could never again be found.

At last he pulled away from her, but the spell still hovered in the air around them, binding them together. "I think I love you," he breathed.

She let her eyes speak for her.

They sat for a long moment just staring at each other.

"So, this must be the young lady you swept off her feet," a voice boomed behind them.

Startled, Faye turned around to see a tall man who looked like an older version of James grinning bemusedly at them.

"Father," James said, jumping to his feet. "Faye, this is my father, King Philip of Aster. Father, allow me to present Faye. She is the one who saved me from drowning yesterday."

"And I am grateful to you for that," the king told her.

She rose shakily to her feet and curtsied as she had seen Sarah do to James.

The king reached out and caught her hand. He bowed over it. "Thank you, my dear, for saving an old man from heartbreak."

She smiled shyly at him. He released her hand and stepped back. "I look forward to seeing you at dinner tonight." He nodded to his son, turned, and left.

"Well, I think he likes you," James said, beaming.

Faye was relieved. She hadn't counted on meeting James's family so soon, at least not until she had had more of a chance to acclimate to her new environment.

"Well, we should get dressed for dinner," James told her.

Surprised, she glanced down at the dress she was wearing.

He laughed. "It's very lovely, but not quite appropriate for this evening. It's to be a very formal dinner. Not only is the duke dining at the castle, but his son, the marquis, has brought his bride-to-be as well. I hear she's lovely, but I'm sure she doesn't hold a candle to you."

As they rose to their feet, Faye's heart was singing. She would do her best to look well for James tonight and to outshine the other ladies present.

"Do you need me to escort you back to your room?"

She shook her head. If she was ever going to familiarize herself with the castle, she might as well start now.

She took her leave of him and made her way carefully to her room. Her legs were much steadier. The only difficulty proved in negotiating the stairs. Still, she kept her hand against the wall to steady herself and moved slowly upward, placing each foot carefully. She sighed in relief when she reached her room.

Amazingly, Sarah was waiting for her with

another gown. It was a brilliant green, brighter than the seaweed that carpeted the ocean. The other woman beamed at Faye's expression.

"I figured you'd be wanting to dress for dinner about now. Looks like I was right."

Faye embraced the woman.

Startled, Sarah gasped and she was sputtering when Faye released her. "Milady," she stammered, "it's not appropriate for you to be doing that."

Faye looked her directly in the eyes.

"You don't care about that, do you?"

Faye shook her head fondly.

Sarah blushed fiercely, but she looked pleased. "Let's get you changed, shall we?"

After what seemed like an eternity, Sarah had finished. She led Faye over to a large cross on the wall. In the middle of the cross a piece of polished glass was set and Faye could see herself in it.

The green of the dress made a stunning contrast against her pale skin. Spots of red decorated each cheek and her lips were red as well, also emphasizing the paleness of the rest of her skin. Her hair shone brightly and had been braided down her back, interwoven with green and gold cord.

"You look like a princess," Sarah said, sighing happily.

I am, Faye thought.

She ran her hand down the material of the dress, liking the way it felt cool and smooth beneath her fingers. Small, brightly colored stones decorated the neckline and glinted brilliantly in the candlelight with a sparkle that matched the one in her eyes. She looked beautiful and she hoped James thought so as well.

At last she was ready. She made her way carefully downstairs, eager to see James. She entered the main hall and saw dozens of people seated around a long table. She saw James instantly. He was looking at someone at the table when a servant whispered something to him. Turning his head, he saw her. He leaped from his seat and came to take her hand.

"You take my breath away," he told her when he was standing before her.

A warm glow suffused her as he took her arm and escorted her to the table. The king welcomed her warmly, and James helped her to her seat. Servants with food appeared from out of nowhere, and soon the feasting had begun.

The variety of food was amazing to her. At home they ate a variety of plant life as well as some of the larger predators of the sea when they happened into mer-kin waters.

Faye took her first bite of something someone called "chicken." It was delicious and had a texture unlike anything she had ever eaten. *It tastes like nothing I've ever known.* She was about to take another bite when the hairs on the back of her neck stood on end.

Slowly she lifted her eyes and found another

staring at her. With a shock she realized that it was Adriana. The other girl was only a few seats away. Her pale skin stood out in dark contrast to her black velvet gown. Her silver hair tumbled over her shoulders. Around her neck she wore a large pearl, dark and shimmering. *I've seen a pearl like that somewhere,* Faye thought. *Where . . . ?*

"How do you like it?" James asked.

Faye turned her attention from Adriana back to James. She smiled and patted her stomach to show her pleasure.

"Good," he said, and laughed. He began to heap her plate with all varieties of exotic foods, bidding her to try first this, then that.

When she got a chance to look back at Adriana, the other was deep in conversation with the dark-haired man next to her. *How strange that she should be here!* It made sense, though, since she had been with the prince in the boat before it had sunk.

She would have to find a way to see her later, alone. Did she know who she was, or had she forgotten her childhood days as a mermaid? Maybe she, too, had visited the Sea Witch in order to ensnare the man seated beside her. That made no sense, though. Adriana had disappeared when she was four. Faye herself had only vague memories of the other mermaid. She wouldn't even have recognized her if it weren't for Kale having identified her yesterday. In fact, the only real thing she remembered about Adriana was seeing her just before she disappeared. The events of that day had been seared into her mind.

"It amazes me, milady that both you and my soon-to-be daughter-in-law bear such a striking resemblance to each other," an older gentleman remarked.

Startled, Faye glanced at him.

"Yes, it is rather remarkable," James commented. "Truly, Robert and I are blessed to have such beauties by our side."

Faye turned to James, but his eyes were fixed on Adriana. She turned to look at Adriana and noticed that the other girl was staring at James, looking flustered and upset.

"A toast," the king called, interrupting the silent exchange. "To women in general for their beauty and mystery, and to Pearl and Faye for gracing us tonight with their presence and reminding us what life is all about."

"Pearl and Faye." All the others at the table lifted their glasses toward the two girls and then drank. Faye imitated the gesture and she and Adriana—*they must call her Pearl*—toasted each other.

For a long minute the two stared at each other. *Does she know me?* Faye wondered. *Does she even know herself?* The man beside Adriana said something and she turned to him.

Faye turned her attention back to James, who was now extolling the virtues of something called "peacock." She spent the rest of dinner listening to him talk and trying to communicate in turn. By the time dinner had ended, she was exhausted.

James walked her back to her room at the end of dinner and gave her a sweet kiss before taking his leave of her. She sighed deeply as she entered her room. Her eyes were so heavy, she wasn't sure how much longer she could stay awake.

Sarah was there waiting for her and helped her change into clothes appropriate to sleep in. Faye then crawled into the bed, and Sarah covered her over with blankets before blowing out the candle next to the bed and exiting the room with her own candle in hand. No sooner had Sarah's candle disappeared than Faye was asleep.

Faye sat bolt upright screaming a silent scream into the darkness. There was something desperately wrong with Kale, she could feel it more strongly than she had ever felt anything. She threw back her coverings and slid out of bed. The stone floor was cold against her feet, and she shivered.

She left her room and padded down the hallway. She wasn't sure where she was going, but the overwhelming need to go somewhere consumed her. Because it was late and everyone should be asleep, she walked as quietly as she could so she wouldn't disturb anyone.

As she moved down another corridor she heard muffled voices, proof that someone other than she was awake. She kept walking.

"—kill the king."

She stopped in her tracks, her heart beginning to pound. Had she heard correctly?

A second voice, older than the first, said, "Everything is in place, but we must tread carefully. I believe James is suspicious."

The younger man chuckled. "James is too taken with the girl to think about anything else. Lucky for us she just came along."

"Yes, lucky," the older man answered, sounding thoughtful. "We'd best rest now. We have much to do in the morning."

The sound of heavy boots on the floor sent her scurrying back down the corridor and around a corner. The owner of the boots must have gone down the corridor in the opposite direction, for the sound began to recede.

Faye peeked around the corner and saw a man's retreating back. She waited a moment before beginning to follow him. She held her breath as she dashed past the door to the room where he had been talking with the other man.

After a couple of more turns in the corridor, the man paused at the top of a narrow, twisting flight of stairs. He glanced toward it as though debating whether he wanted to go down it. Then he shook his head and walked on.

The hairs on the back of Faye's neck lifted, and once the man was out of sight she hurried down the stairs. They swirled deeper and deeper into darkness, lit only by torches placed at intervals. At last they opened into a long, narrow hall lined on both sides by cages.

She shuddered. She had seen cages before, lying at the bottom of the ocean among wreckages of ships. She had once seen a whole group of lobsters in one, their lifeless bodies a grim testament to the methods of man.

She slowly walked down the hall. The cages on either side of her were empty. At the far end, though, she thought she caught a glimmer of movement, a flash of something white.

She reached the last cage and saw a man standing inside. He turned his head slowly toward her. Kale! She lunged forward, reaching through the bars to touch him. *What is he doing here?* she wondered, taking in his human form.

"Faye?" he asked.

She opened her mouth to tell him it was she, but no sound would come out. She nodded fiercely instead.

"Faye, is that really you? These hands feel like yours," he said, carefully feeling them with his fingertips.

Confused, she stared at him. *How can he not recognize me?*

"The Witch took my sight. I can't see you. Speak to me, please," he begged.

His skin was pale, almost glowing in the darkness around him. It made the bruises around his left eye stand out all the more, dark and ugly.

Tears of frustration filled her eyes. She should have known that the Witch's magic would come with a price for him as well. She lifted one of her hands and placed a finger across his lips.

"Do we need to be quiet?" he whispered.

She took both her hands and placed one on either side of his head. Gently, she shook his head back and forth. Then she took his hand and guided it through the bars. His hand was also bruised and there was blood beneath his fingernails. She took his index finger and placed it against her shoulder and then lifted it and laid it across her lips.

Understanding lit his face. "You can't speak?"

With his finger still across her lips, she nodded her head.

"The Witch took your voice and my eyes?"

Again, she nodded.

"I understand."

She moved his hand from her lips and held it between hers. She moved both their hands to one of the bars, wrapped his and her hand around it, and shook it hard.

"I haven't been able to find a way out," he told her. "I'm not even sure where I am or why I'm here. I was talking with Adriana on the beach. They call her Pearl here. She had to leave, and just a few moments later some men grabbed me. I don't know how many there were, or what they wanted. They just told me I was under arrest for crimes I had committed 'against His Majesty's subjects.' They hit me in the head, and the next thing I knew I woke up here."

Her eyes began to fill with water and it startled her. A few fat drops fell and slid down her cheeks. She knelt down slowly and touched his legs.

"I did it for you and Adriana. I had to see her, to try to bring her home. More importantly, though, I had to make sure you were safe."

More water found its way down her cheeks as she stood back up. She grasped both his hands and methodically lifted seven of his fingers into the air. She left them alone for a moment, and then firmly pushed one of the seven down.

"Yes," he answered softly. "I had seven days as well. Now, it seems, only six remain."

She drew her finger across his throat.

"And then we die."

They stood for a moment, the silence stretching between them. At last, Kale spoke. "Have you found the human you came here to be with?"

She grasped his head and nodded it.

"Does he care for you?"

She nodded his head again.

He breathed a sigh of relief. "That's good. Now, if only I could find Pearl."

She pulled his hand to touch her shoulder again and then moved his fingers to gently touch her eyes.

"You've seen her?"

She nodded.

"Where is she?"

She took his hands, spread them slightly, and then waved them toward the ground.

"You mean she's here?" he asked excitedly.

She moved his hands back to her head and nodded.

"Please bring her to see me."

She wanted to tell him that she would try, that she would do her best, but she was at a loss as to how to express it. So, she grasped his hands and squeezed them, praying that he would understand.

"You should go now," he told her. "I don't think it would be good for them to find you here."

He was right, although she wished he wasn't. She gave his hands a final squeeze before dropping them and moving away reluctantly. She couldn't bear to see him caged, and her heart ached for him. The best thing she could do for him, though, was find a way to communicate with Pearl.

She turned and left, moving back up the stairs, stopping every so often to listen for the sounds of anyone approaching. There was nothing, though. When she reached the top of the stairs she felt a little more at ease, but she still raced through the corridors until she made her way back to her own room.

Once inside she collapsed on her bed in relief. Her hours of life were slipping away; she could feel them going one by one, leading her closer to death. Now she held Kale's fate in her hands as well, and his life was slipping through her fingers. She had to find a way to communicate with Pearl. If Pearl and James did not agree to marry them, then she and Kale were dead.

She fell asleep and dreamed of the lobster cages by the wreckage of the boat. Only instead of the decaying bodies of lobsters, it contained the bodies of herself and Kale.

❖ Chapter Eight ❖

At last she was standing before Father Gregory. Robert reached out and took her hand. The touch of his skin sent cold chills through her. She stared into his eyes, searching them for a spark of warmth, but there was nothing except the glittering ice. This then was her fate, her destiny.

"My betrothed?" Pearl asked, a kaleidoscope of emotions rushing through her.

"Yes, child. The Marq—Robert, came by to ask for your hand."

"And you said yes?"

"Of course we did," Mary spoke up. She moved to Pearl and wrapped her arms around her.

"Why me?" she asked. Of all the questions burning in her mind, that one stood out.

Robert smiled. "A long time I have watched you from afar, admiring you. You are so beautiful and so kind. I know my cousin, James, thinks the world of you."

"He didn't want me to have to marry the blacksmith," Pearl breathed, realization dawning.

Robert shook his head. "No, he did not. I am in need of a wife, and you a husband. I hope you don't think me too fanciful, but I love you. It was James who gave me the courage to come forward and tell you, and ask for your hand."

"He said he would try to help me."

Robert touched her cheek gently. "Nay, it is me he has helped, though I pray that this will make you happy as well. I promise to be a good husband and to do everything in my power to make you love me as I love you."

Mary put her hand on Pearl's shoulder. "It's the miracle I've been praying for," she whispered, for Pearl's ears alone.

Pearl had no words.

"Well, we'd best be off before the hour grows any later," Robert said, taking Pearl's elbow.

Mary picked up a basket and handed it to Pearl. "Here are some of your things. We'll bring anything else you need the day after tomorrow."

"But . . . what?" Pearl asked, looking from Mary to Finneas.

"The prince thought it would be a good idea if my fiancée came to the castle now," Robert explained, "to start the wedding preparations. Your parents will follow in a couple of days so that your mother can be with you."

Mary smoothed a strand of hair back from Pearl's face. "Just imagine, dear: A week from today you will be a bride."

The words chilled her to the bone. One look at

Mary's earnest face, though, and she didn't know what to say to her. She was spared from having to answer by a voice at the door.

"Milord," a guard addressed Robert.

"What is it?"

"We have captured the murderer!"

"Excellent," Robert replied as Mary breathed an audible sigh of relief. "Where did you find him?"

"On the beach not ten minutes from here. He was half dressed and blind."

"Blind, but how can that be?" asked Mary.

"In the struggle with the last girl, she was able to throw fabric dye in his eyes. It has apparently hurt his vision."

"Murderer?" Pearl asked, panicking. "What is all this about?"

Finneas nodded. "There's a man, not right in the head, been attacking women up and down the coast. He killed the last one two villages over. Apparently he's looking for someone named Adriana. He meets pretty girls and then tells them he knew them from birth."

"Oh my," she breathed, sinking to a seat at the table.

"Aye, it's a terrible thing," Mary answered.

"There's no need to worry, my darling. He'll be dealt with swiftly. I assure you that you are quite safe," Robert vowed.

She forced a shaky laugh. "He sounds like a monster."

"He would have to be to do the things he's been doing. But we needn't worry about him, not when we have so many more pleasant things to think about." Robert turned to Finneas and Mary. "And now I'm afraid we really must take our leave."

"We will see you in two days," Finneas confirmed.

Pearl rose to her feet, taking the basket Mary had packed for her. Outside, Robert patted the neck of a beautiful white mare. "Have you ridden before?"

"No," she confessed.

He flicked the reins over the horse's head and handed them to one of his companions. "Well then, best you ride with me this time."

He moved over to the side of a massive stallion. The animal's gray coat glistened. In one fluid motion, Robert mounted the beast. He extended his hand down to her. "Put your foot on mine and I'll help you up."

She did as she was told, placing her right foot on top of his riding boot. She hopped twice and then he pulled her up, helping her twist in midair. She found herself seated sideways on the horse in front of Robert. He put his arms around her and gathered up the reins.

He clucked, and the horse began to walk. Another cluck, and the mighty animal eased into a canter. The three-beat rhythm was unnerving as was the feeling of the wind stinging her eyes. She felt fragile, exposed, as though she could topple any moment to her death beneath the churning hooves.

Robert's arms tightened around her. "I've got you," he reassured her.

Somehow, that didn't make her feel much better. Still, the ride passed swiftly, and soon the horses' hooves were clattering on the cobblestones in the castle courtyard.

The castle took her breath away. It was magnificent, and larger even than she had imagined. Dozens of times she had dreamed of seeing it, but never quite like this, in the arms of another man and a stranger at that.

Servants ran up to take the reins. Robert dismounted and then put his hands on her waist and lifted her down to the ground. She grabbed his arm for a moment to balance herself and then stepped away. He let his hands drop.

"The banquet won't start for about another half hour. You'll just have time to change, if you hurry."

"But I have nothing to change into."

He smiled. "They should have something that will suit you."

Two women rushed up to them. One, with a cheerful smile and round cheeks, exclaimed, "Dear heavens, we just have young ladies sprouting up all over today!"

"Sisters, I'd wager, from the looks of it," the other affirmed.

"I have no sister," Pearl told her, her stomach twisting into knots. *Faye! Is she really here? What if that part of Kale's story is true?* Her head swam; too much had happened in too little time. She didn't know what to think or whom to believe.

"Well, then there is a resemblance, but I reckon you to be far prettier than she is," the first woman said with a wink.

Pearl couldn't help but smile; the woman's enthusiasm was infectious. "I was told I needed to change for dinner?" she questioned.

"Mercy, yes. I'm Sarah, and this is Martha. She'll help you find something real fine."

The next thing Pearl knew, Martha had whisked her off to a bedroom three times the size of the cottage that had been her only home. *At least the only one I remember.* She shuddered as her thoughts returned to Kale.

How could he be a murderer? He seemed so gentle, so kind. She trembled as she remembered the kiss they'd shared. Then he had spoken those words "I am your betrothed." What had he meant by that? He hadn't been the only one to say those words to her today, though.

She wanted to laugh at the irony. A week ago she had had no prospects as far as finding a husband. Now, she had three proposals: the blacksmith, the murderer, and the nobleman.

Faster than she would have thought possible, Martha produced a gown of exquisite beauty. As Martha helped her dress, her thoughts turned to Robert. *Who was he?* She had never seen him before or heard James speak of him.

James must have approved, though, if he told Robert to bring me to the castle, she realized. But if James had known that Robert intended to marry her, why had he acted so strangely yesterday? She thought back on the events. He had said he had found an answer to her dilemma about marrying the blacksmith. She had thought when he took her out in the boat that he was going to propose. *He must have been going to tell me about Robert instead.*

"What kind of man is Robert?" she asked Martha.

"He's a nobleman, a marquis."

"Yes, but what *kind* of man is he? Is he compassionate?"

"I don't know, milady, I've only seen him a couple of times."

"You must have heard something, though," she pressed.

"I've heard he's a great warrior. His father, the duke, owns extensive lands to the east and is a second cousin to the king."

"Robert said he and James were cousins," Pearl mused.

Martha glanced up at her with a look of horror on her face. Pearl flushed, realizing that she shouldn't have called the prince by his name. She was saved from an explanation when Sarah bustled into the room.

"There you are, looking mighty handsome at that. How wonderful it will be to have two such ladies dining in the castle tonight!"

Martha finished with the hem of the dress and moved back. Sarah walked around her and looked her up and down. Pearl felt uncomfortable being on display.

"Well, you do look lovely. Now, let's go. We don't want to be late."

Trepidation filled Pearl's heart as she followed Martha from the room and down to the main floor. She nervously fingered the black velvet of her gown. She had never before worn such a fine garment. *I don't belong here!* she thought, fear gripping her. *This is James's world, not mine.* When she entered the hall, Robert was the first person she saw. He moved forward quickly, a smile lighting his face.

"You are a vision. The angels must weep gazing upon your beauty."

Pearl dropped her eyes. "Thank you, milord."

"To you, I am just Robert."

"Thank you, Robert."

He took her hand and led her to the table. They stopped before an older man, and Robert introduced her. "Pearl, this is my father, Stephen, duke of Novan. Father, this is Pearl, my fiancée."

"My dear, it is a great honor to meet you and to welcome you into my family," the duke assured her as he kissed her hand.

Before Pearl could reply, there was a rustling sound as everyone who was already seated at the table rose. At the far end of the room, King Philip and Prince James entered. They moved to the head of the table and took their seats.

James looked as she had never seen him, dressed in all the finery of his station. At that moment she realized how he had always dressed down in her presence, even when he was in the market and was wearing princely clothes.

Everyone else sat, and Robert helped her to her seat. James was looking around the room as though he was expecting to see somebody in particular. At last his eyes fell on her and widened in surprise. *Pearl,* he mouthed.

She nodded her head. They were close enough to speak to each other, but she didn't have the words. He, too, seemed at a loss. A servant scuttled forward and whispered something to him. James turned his head suddenly toward one of the Hall's entrances, and Pearl turned as well.

There in the door was a young woman in a gown of deepest green. Long, silver hair fell in a braid down the center of her back. Her face was like delicate porcelain.

James rose hurriedly and went to her. She took his hand, and he led her back to the banquet table where room had been saved for her. As she sat down, Pearl noticed the adoring look that she was giving James.

Faye! It has to be. That part of Kale's story, at least, is true. Her head began to spin. Too much was happening too quickly and it was all turning into a blur in her mind.

Realizing she was staring, Pearl forced her attention back to the table and to Robert. Just then, food began to appear, and though she did not feel very hungry, she was grateful for the distraction.

"The king's chef is the finest in the land," Robert told her. "I hate to admit that, for our own is quite excellent. I am afraid you will be altogether spoiled, though, by the time we get home."

"Home." It was a strange word to hear from his lips, knowing that it was to be his home as well. For thirteen years her home had been with Mary and Finneas; before that, she had no idea. What would home be like with Robert and the duke?

She glanced up to stare once more at Faye. After a moment the other girl lifted her head and looked at her. A look of surprise crossed her face as though she recognized her. Just then James said something, and Faye turned away again.

Pearl dropped her own eyes with a sigh. She found herself picking at a bird that rather resembled a goose. It was really quite good, and she wished she had more of an appetite so that she could enjoy it.

"That's peacock," Robert informed her. "The female is a brown color, and the male is bright blue with brightly colored tail feathers."

He went on to point out other exotic foods on the table. When a tray of fish was offered her, she drew back slightly. Robert waved his hand, and the servant removed it.

"I apologize, you have probably eaten enough fish

in your life to never want to eat it again," Robert said solicitously.

She looked at him gratefully. "I really don't care to eat fish at all."

"Then you don't have to, not now, not ever," he said.

Soon, Robert was lost in the food and they both ate quietly. From time to time she could feel James's eyes upon her, but, for the most part he seemed intent on the other woman.

A wave of loneliness swept over her. Mary and Finneas were home, asleep by now, and James, the only other person she knew, might as well have been a world away. She swallowed the lump in her throat and instead spooned a piece of fish onto her plate. Robert noticed and raised an eyebrow but didn't ask.

The fish sat there while she stared at it. She wondered if Finneas had caught it and if Mary had prepared it for market. In truth, she had no intention of eating it. It was the little piece of home she needed, though. Everything was happening so fast, and the people she most depended on were not available for her to talk to. When at last one of the servants took away her plate with the fish still on it, she felt bereft, alone, and naked.

Soon after that, diners began to leave the table. She made her excuses to Robert and hurried up to her room, wanting more than anything to be alone. She undressed swiftly and donned the sleeping gown that Martha had left out for her.

She was exhausted, but sleep wouldn't come easily.

Too much had happened in too short a time. Her mind kept going over the events of the day, seeking some kind of meaning out of it all.

Where had Kale come from? Was he really a murderer? Remembering the kiss they had shared on the beach made her cheeks burn in the darkness. She couldn't believe that a murderer could kiss that way. *Not that I'd know anything about kisses*, she thought as she rolled onto her side.

She had known Kale less than an hour and he had kissed her. She couldn't believe he'd had the audacity. Worse still, she couldn't believe that she had let him. Why, then, had time seemed to stand still when he'd kissed her? And why did she find herself holding her breath when she remembered it?

Then again, she had known Robert for less than a minute and she was engaged to him. He hadn't tried to kiss her yet, even though in a week he would have the right to far more than that from her.

She blushed more fiercely thinking about the wedding night. She had thought of marriage in the past, but never that aspect of it. Her stomach twisted in nervous knots, and she couldn't help but wish that it would be James, or even Kale, whom she would give herself to.

But James was going to marry Faye, the woman who had saved his life. And Kale, she didn't know where Kale was, but he was probably imprisoned somewhere. *I wonder what's going to happen to him. Could he have really done those terrible things?*

She fell asleep, and the nightmares came back stronger. Only now she watched as James kissed Faye. A hand touched her shoulder, and she turned around to see Robert staring at her. He bent down to kiss her, and over his shoulder she saw Kale staring at her.

She closed her eyes so she would not have to see him, and kissed Robert.

The next day was the busiest in Pearl's life. For three hours in the morning she was subjected to the not-so-delicate ministrations of the royal seamstress. The woman draped her with various fabrics, took measurements four times, and even managed to stab Pearl's ankle with one of her needles.

The blood horrified the seamstress more than it did Pearl, though: The woman had turned ash white and muttered apologies for five minutes. Pearl just stared at her, bewildered. *Does she actually think I'm going to do anything to her?* she wondered.

No sooner had the woman left than Sarah was dressing her in a garment much simpler than the velvet one of the night before, which was still more elegant than anything she had ever owned. The dress was scarlet, and as Pearl looked at herself in the reflective glass in her room she couldn't help but think back to earlier in the week when she had viewed the white of her skin against the red of the tomato she'd bought at market. *Now I'm wearing the tomato,* she thought with a shake of her head.

Once dressed, she was escorted downstairs by the excited maid. Robert was waiting for her in the hall. Walking up to him, she had to admit herself that he was very handsome.

"I thought you could use some fresh air after your busy morning," he told her. "I thought a picnic would be in order. It will also give us a chance to talk, get to know each other better."

"That would be nice," she said, warming to him slightly. He did seem to be thoughtful.

He held out his arm to her, and she took it. Together they walked toward the door. Halfway there, James walked through it, and Pearl felt her heart stop for a moment.

He looked at her, mouth slightly open as though he was about to say something. Then he closed it and dipped his head in acknowledgment.

"Robert . . . Pearl."

"Highness," Robert responded.

"James," Pearl whispered, her mouth having gone dry.

He took a step closer. He looked like he wanted to say something, and she wished he would, anything to break the dreadful silence that suddenly surrounded them.

Finally he spoke, and his voice sounded hoarse to her. "I want to take this opportunity to congratulate you both. Robert, there is no finer woman than Pearl."

"A happy fact that I am well-acquainted with," Robert answered.

"Pearl . . . the two of you are a handsome pair," James said, staring deeply into her eyes.

There was something shining in his eyes, but she couldn't read it. There was more that he wasn't saying. Frustrated, she nodded to acknowledge that he had spoken.

He straightened up. "I wish the two of you all the happiness that this world has to offer."

"We are most grateful for your wishes, Highness."

James nodded and then smiled in a pained manner. "I shall not keep you."

He left swiftly, and Robert patted her hand. "I thank God he gave me the courage to ask you," Robert said, loudly enough that James could hear. "Shall we be on our way?"

"Yes."

The picnic was pleasant, but at the end of it Pearl felt like she knew Robert no better than she had the day before. He told her stories of his childhood and of tournaments he had entered and won. Some of the stories were heroic, some funny, but there was something lacking in all of them. She had no sense of his true personality, his morals, his soul. That worried her.

On the way back to the castle they rode through the center of the village, Pearl sitting before him on his steed. He wrapped an arm possessively around her waist. Pearl had been used to inciting stares and whispers her entire life, but nothing like this. Several people actually began cheering.

I lived a simple life, as a fisherman's daughter, and they despised and feared me. Now that I am marrying a marquis, they treat me as one of their own, she thought bitterly.

Still, she couldn't help but feel a twinge of satisfaction when the mother of the boy she had saved from the runaway cart looked up at her with a mixture of awe and jealousy on her face.

"Would you mind if we stop and speak with Father Gregory for a moment?" Robert asked her suddenly.

The mention of Father Gregory made Pearl suddenly feel nauseated. Talking to the good father would make it all too real. Still, she forced herself to say, "No, I won't mind."

Robert pulled the steed up in front of the church. He dismounted in one fluid motion and helped her down as well. He flipped the reins over the horse's head and let them dangle toward the ground. The mighty beast made a chuffing sound and shifted his weight onto three legs.

Robert patted the horse's neck before taking Pearl's arm and leading her into the church.

Father Gregory had already heard the news and was beaming from ear to ear as he greeted them. She twisted her pearl between her fingers as Robert and Father Gregory talked. Within a minute the time for the ceremony had been set and her fate had been sealed.

Exiting the church, Pearl was shocked to see

Thomas kneeling next to Robert's horse.

"Can I help you, sir?" Robert asked, sounding equally surprised.

The blacksmith rose slowly. He turned and faced them. "Your horse looked like one of his shoes was working itself loose." He held up his hammer. "He should be good for a couple more days now, but I'll need to check all his shoes."

"Thank you," Robert replied. "I'll see that one of my servants brings him to you in the morning."

Thomas nodded. He stared at the ground for a moment and twisted his hands about his hammer. At last he looked up again and looked Pearl in the eyes. "My pleasure."

"What do I owe you?" Robert asked.

"No charge, milord. Consider it a wedding present. Good luck to you both."

Shame flooded Pearl. Thomas was a good man, he deserved better than this. She didn't know what to say, though.

Robert saved her. "Thank you and good day to you, blacksmith," he said, before hoisting Pearl up onto the saddle. He mounted behind her, and in a moment they were off, leaving behind the blacksmith, the village, and everything she had ever known.

Back at the castle she had yet another meeting with the seamstress and then she met with the cook and the baker. Last, she spoke with a woman about decorations. By the time dinner was being served, she hardly felt like going down. Sarah dressed her, though, and sent her on her way.

The food was just as extravagant as it had been the night before and, just like the night before, she found she had little stomach for it. After dinner she dragged herself back upstairs and quickly fell asleep.

She dreamed that a woman came into her room and shook her shoulders, trying to wake her. Pearl just swatted at her hands and rolled over. Soon the woman disappeared, and Pearl began to dream again, this time the old dreams—and they were just as disturbing as always.

✤ Chapter Nine ✤

Mary quaked as the footman helped her into the coach. Finneas climbed in after her and sat on the seat across from her, looking as nervous as she felt. Neither of them had ever been to the castle before and weren't sure what to expect.

The carriage started with a slight jolt, and Finneas smiled wanly at her.

"How do you think our Pearl is doing?" she asked Finneas.

He smiled. "I imagine she is well."

She had known him long enough, though, to read beyond the smile, and the look in his eyes was one of worry.

She was worried too. She didn't know anything about the marquis or his father, the duke. *At least it's not the blacksmith,* she reminded herself. She just prayed that Pearl was happy. The marquis seemed like a nice enough man, and he could offer Pearl so much.

They reached the castle in short order and were escorted quickly through it to their room. She heard Finneas muttering beside her the entire way.

The walls were of great stone blocks, the same as

the rest of the castle. They were covered in tapestries, and the floors were covered with fur rugs. There was a large bed, two small sitting tables with chairs, and a standing wardrobe. A window in the room gave a view of the village.

The servant deposited their bags and, bowing, began to leave.

"Excuse me, could you tell us where to find our daughter, Pearl?" Mary asked before the man could leave.

"I will tell her that you have arrived, ma'am," the man said. "Dinner will be served in a quarter of an hour." He bowed and then exited.

"It's bigger than our whole house," Finneas noted.

"It's bigger than three of our houses," Mary corrected him.

"It's too big. What does one do with all this space?"

She shrugged her shoulders. "I have no idea." She moved around, inspecting the bed and the other furniture. Everything was heavy-looking, made out of the finest wood.

"I guess we should go find the Hall," Finneas noted.

Mary nodded, and they went out in search of dinner.

Mary was exhausted. She couldn't remember ever eating so much. As overwhelming as the food had been, though, sitting at the same table as the king had been more so. She sighed, looking down at her dress. She had been sadly out of fashion, especially compared with Pearl and the girl called Faye.

"What do you think is going to be expected of us as the parents of a marquesa?" she now asked Finneas, back in their room.

He shrugged his shoulders. "I have no idea. Personally, I just hope to be left alone in our own little house."

She rolled her eyes at him in a teasing fashion. Finneas was plainspoken, and she knew he had been ill at ease all during dinner.

"What did you think of Faye?" she asked.

He stopped pacing and looked at her. "I think she reminded me a lot of our daughter," he said warily, taking a step closer to her.

"Me too. You don't think . . ."

"That there's a connection?" Finneas asked. "I don't know, but it makes me nervous."

"We always assumed that Pearl was one of a kind, unique."

"And now we're both wondering, 'What if she isn't?'"

Mary nodded.

He shook his head. "We have to ask Pearl what she knows of her."

Mary laughed nervously. "It's strange, but after all these years, I almost don't want to know."

"I understand," he said softly. "We know what we

both think. Either we're about to lose everything we've believed for so long, or . . ."

"Or have it confirmed for us," she breathed.

Silence stretched between them. In their hearts they had always believed that Pearl wasn't entirely human. Neither knew for sure what she was, but the thought of finding out was a bit overwhelming. *Sometimes it's better to guess at the truth than know it. Actually, what frightens me more is the thought that we might've been wrong all these years.*

Finneas picked up a candle. "I'm going to take a look around before bed," he told her, exiting the room.

The spell was broken, and she laughed out loud. Whether he would say so or not, she knew he was nervous at the thought of sleeping in a place he did not know.

She heard running steps outside the room and turned just as Pearl burst through the door.

"Mama!"

Pearl ran into her arms and began to sob. Bewildered, Mary just held her and let her cry.

At last, when her tears had dried, Mary sat Pearl down upon the bed. "Now tell me, child, what is it that is bothering you?"

"Mama, there's . . . just so much, I can't . . . ," Pearl choked.

Mary felt tears stinging the back of her eyes. She couldn't stand to see her child in pain. "Try, baby, please—you used to tell me everything. Well, almost everything," she joked, waving a hand at their surroundings.

Pearl smiled a little at that, and it warmed Mary's heart.

"Mama, tell me about that night."

Mary frowned at her. "What night is that?"

"The night you and Papa found me."

Mary sighed. The time for avoiding the topic was over—it had to be, even she knew that. "It was Papa who found you. Why do you want to hear it again?"

"I just do."

Mary's frown deepened. For years she had successfully avoided Pearl's many questions on the topic. She didn't have all the answers. Her Pearl was grown up, though, and the time for questions had come. She wished she felt more prepared, but she wasn't. All she could tell her was what she knew, what she and Finneas had seen. So many nights Pearl had asked her for the details and Mary had skimmed over them. Tonight, though, it might be different, it must be.

Mary sighed and her face grew very still. "It had been a beautiful day, the sun was shining, and the sky was the brightest blue you ever saw. There was not a cloud anywhere in sight. I remember thinking that there had never been such a beautiful day, at least not in my memory." She chuckled. "Even Father Gregory was in a good mood."

Pearl giggled at the mention of the dour old

priest. Mary laughed, and Pearl joined her. Finally, they quieted.

Mary sobered, remembering. "Even the ocean was still, as though it were holding its breath. It was Sunday, so your father didn't take the boat out until after lunch."

Mary stopped, remembering the feeling of trepidation she had when she saw Finneas off that afternoon. The day had been beautiful, but something had seemed amiss to her, something she couldn't explain.

Pearl sat with an expectant look, staring at her for several minutes before prompting, "And then?"

Mary turned to look at her, wincing at the memory. "And then everything changed, in a moment. The sky turned black, and the seas started boiling. The rain began to fall in great sheets, and you couldn't hear anyone speak for the thunder. It was so dark that even the lightning revealed nothing more than a step away from you. Folks say it was the Devil's Storm. It destroyed half a village five days' walk from here. I was in the market and somehow I made my way home, though I have never known how. I sat for hours waiting and praying for Finneas to come home. Finally, a voice told me to go look for him. I walked to the beach and I saw him trying to drag the boat up onto the sand. He had fallen, and the boat was slipping back into the water. I put my hands over his and helped heave the boat backward to safety."

"Father made it home."

She nodded. "And when he did, he wasn't alone."

"I was with him," Pearl breathed.

Mary nodded. "Yes, you were."

"The storm came up so fast, I didn't even have time to start home."

Pearl jumped, and they both turned to see Finneas standing a few feet away. The light from the candle he was carrying cast shadows across his face but did nothing to hide his piercing eyes.

"I started to pull for shore as hard as I could, but the sea only swept me farther out. At one point I was sure I was going to die. I prayed to God to take care of Mary. It was at that point that I saw a light in the water. I thought an angel was coming to take me. I rowed over and looked down in the water. I saw an angel—just not the kind I was expecting. I saw a little girl treading water."

Finneas moved and sat down on Pearl's other side. "Your hair was floating on top of the water, glowing. I pulled you into the boat. You weren't wearing a stitch of clothing, and when I tried to wrap a wet blanket around you, you just cried and threw it off. Then I began to row again, harder than before. I knew God did not want me to die on that ocean. He would not have led me to find you if He didn't want me to take you to shore. Eventually we made it to the beach. Mary found us and we ran home."

"I couldn't believe what I was seeing," Mary continued. "You looked about four. Everything about you was small and delicate except your legs, I've never seen legs that long on a child."

"And your eyes," Finneas added. "They were so big, and such a dark blue-black."

"When Finneas set you down you didn't move, and you were so pale that I thought you were dead, drowned. But then you looked up at me and said something I couldn't understand. You didn't speak English. Not a word for almost an entire season. And then, when you did speak, the first word you said was 'Papa.' Then you spoke naturally, like you'd been learning all those words and saving them up."

"Your skin was so pale," Finneas added, "that when you held your hand up to the fire, it was as though I could see through it. We both could."

"We told everyone that you were the child of one of my cousins who lived in the village that was destroyed by the storm," Mary explained.

"And this pearl?" Pearl questioned, fingering it.

"You had that clutched tightly in your fist. I couldn't get it away from you until you fell asleep and your hand loosened," Mary explained.

Pearl sat quietly, as though she was absorbing the information. "Do you think I'm human?"

Mary shook her head slowly. "I don't know," she said, her voice a whisper. "I've never known and, God forgive me, I've never wanted to know."

"It was safer that way," Finneas explained.

"The truth is, we didn't know and we didn't care if you weren't. We just knew that we were happy to have you, our darling little girl, and we weren't going to let any harm come to you. Finneas was meant to find you, I have always believed that. We were meant to protect you, and I will believe that until my dying day."

"There's a young man and another girl, they look like me," Pearl confided.

"I saw the girl, Faye, earlier at dinner," Mary told her. "I noticed the resemblance and I confess I wondered if she was somehow related to you."

"What about this man?" Finneas asked.

"I found him, a couple days ago, sitting by the sea. He claimed to know me, that I had been kidnapped as a child and he had been searching for me ever since."

"Not the man they caught who's been killing women?" Finneas asked, horrified.

Pearl nodded. "I haven't known what to think. I *do* know that what he said to me had the ring of truth to it."

Mary exchanged a glance with Finneas. It could be true, but the thought frightened her. What if their Pearl left? Worse, what if more people came looking for her and whoever kidnapped her was among them? "Have you heard where they're keeping him?" she asked.

Pearl shook her head, and Mary sighed. "Then we'll cross that bridge when we come to it."

Mary felt as though she'd blinked and three days had passed. She and Martha had become great friends, and had taken over all the preparations for the wedding. She spent a whole day discussing the wedding banquet with the chef who was a delightful man. He even gave Mary some cooking tips that she planned on using at home.

Martha had made Pearl's wedding gown and it was beautiful, made of pale blue silk. Mary cried when Pearl tried it on for size.

Finneas spent his time scowling around and looking generally uncomfortable. If only Pearl were happier, Mary would have found the whole adventure wonderful. She hadn't been able to get the thought out of her head that Pearl might have been kidnapped as a child. That, coupled with the fact that Faye could very well be connected to Pearl's past, added to her unrest.

She made her way to Pearl's room to wake her for her final fitting. "Tomorrow is the big day," she told Pearl as she woke her.

There were dark circles under Pearl's eyes that stood out in sharp contrast against her skin. "Are you all right?" Mary asked, sitting down beside her.

"I'm just having bad dreams," Pearl said.

Mary's heart filled with great sympathy. "It's normal to feel anxious before your wedding," she assured her. "Why, I didn't sleep for three days before I married your father."

"Truly?" Pearl asked. "Were you nervous?"

"Incredibly," Mary confided. "I worried about all manner of things, but mostly whether I was making a huge mistake."

"But you didn't."

"No, I didn't. Your father is a wonderful man and I couldn't be happier." She gave Pearl's shoulder a squeeze. "It will work out for you, too. Now, up with you and let's get this dress tried on."

She beamed as Pearl pulled the garment over her head minutes later. She looked radiant and grown up. Her Pearl was a woman.

Things are going even better than planned, Robert thought with satisfaction. As the manservant was putting the final touches on his wedding clothes, he couldn't help but chuckle in satisfaction.

His father sat across the room, waiting for the servant to finish and leave. The two of them had much to discuss.

For the past five days he had managed to keep Pearl and James from speaking to each other, lest either figure out his deception. He felt a momentary twinge of regret. Pearl really was a remarkable woman. Perhaps if he had met her under other circumstances . . . he shook his head. Under other circumstances he never would have looked at her since she was a commoner. No, she was just part of the game he and his father had been playing for months. A game that would win them the throne.

It had been Robert's spies who had first discovered the unique relationship between Pearl and James. It had been his intention to find some way to exploit it, though the current turn of events surprised even him. Still, things were working out well. The prince was uneasy and off-balance. That made him vulnerable, and a decade of tournaments had taught Robert how to exploit vulnerability.

His father had been planning for years to kill King Philip and seize the throne. The day after next, years of planning would start to pay off. It was a shame, really, that he wasn't going to have an opportunity to have Pearl in his bed. She would be dead before sundown, though.

The servant finished and, bowing, left the room. After a minute, Robert crossed to his father.

"Everything is in place," the duke said, a wicked gleam in his eye. "In the morning, a dangerous criminal will escape and poison the king."

"The killer's connection to the prince will be discovered, and he will be killed."

"And after the others are dead, the throne will be ours."

Robert picked up a wine goblet from the table. "I'll drink to that," he said, and downed the clarrey in one swallow.

The duke lifted a glass as well. "Here's to us: What a fine pair of widowers we will be."

❧ Chapter Ten ❧

Dearly beloved, we are gathered here in the eyes of God and these witnesses to join Robert and Pearl in holy matrimony. If there is anyone here who knows of any reason why these two should not be joined, let him speak now or forever hold his peace.

It was the day before her wedding. Pearl fingered the fabric of her gown where it was hanging and wondered what the morrow would bring. There was nothing left for her to do. Between Mary and the servant, Martha, everything had been taken out of her hands. There was nothing left for her to do but wait.

She realized that it was one of the only times she had been alone since entering the castle. Robert was being fitted for his wedding clothes, else she was sure he would be with her. He had been her constant companion for the past several days.

She wandered the castle, seeing all the places where James had played as a child. This was home to him and, after tomorrow, could never be for her. From the looks of things, it would, however, be home to Faye.

Faye. She had seen the girl at every turn she had

made the last few days, but always there had been others around, and before she could speak to her, Faye would have disappeared again. Pearl felt convinced, though, that Faye always looked as though she was about to speak, or at least try to. *Does she want to see me about something?* Pearl wondered. If she did, she obviously didn't want others to be around when she approached her. *If she's going to marry James, maybe she's just curious about me, or worried that I'm competition.* Pearl snorted to herself. There was little worry about the last. With Faye around, James hadn't even given her a second glance. *So much for friendship.* She sighed. At least she knew he wasn't in love with her. That made it a little easier to marry Robert, knowing that she never could have had James's heart.

Still, there was one who did love her, or claimed to, at any rate. She couldn't help but wonder what had happened to Kale. Where had the guards taken him? She felt sorry for him. From him her thoughts returned to Faye. The two seemed so alike, somehow. It was more than just their startling physical attributes, so similar to her own. It just seemed strange that one was blind and the other mute.

On one of the few occasions that she had seen Faye she had observed the girl trying to speak. That was not the action of someone mute from birth. Kale had also claimed that his blindness had come on suddenly, within twenty-four hours of their meeting. *Our official meeting, at any rate,* she thought, remembering his claim to have seen her the day before while she was swimming for shore.

She stopped, noting one of the finer tapestries in the corridor she was walking. It was a picture of the ocean with a mermaid sitting on a rock in the middle of it. Young men were sailing their ship toward her. *Mermaid as temptress.* It was an interesting story. She sighed and continued on her walk.

She heard a footstep behind her in the hall and she turned. Faye darted up to her swiftly, her enormous eyes bright. Before Pearl could say a word, Faye took her by the hand and motioned for her to follow. Her curiosity piqued, Pearl went along.

Faye moved silently, her steps inaudible on the floor. Pearl's own footfalls were thunderous by comparison. Faye finally turned to her and placed a finger over her lips, signaling for Pearl to be quiet. Pearl nodded understanding.

Faye moved through the corridors as though she had been haunting them all her life. Her head bobbed from side to side as though she was listening for something, or someone.

A chill danced up Pearl's spine. Wherever Faye was taking her, it was clear she didn't want anyone else to discover them. For a brief moment Pearl thought the other girl was luring her somewhere to kill her so she would have no competition. The thought was a silly one, though, and Pearl banished it with a wave of her hand. Not only did the other girl have nothing to fear from her, but Pearl couldn't believe that anyone with such innocent eyes was capable of violence.

They turned down a last corridor and then began descending a flight of stairs. Down they went, farther and farther into the bowels of the castle. Torches lit the way every few feet. Faye glanced back frequently to make sure that she was still following.

At last they reached the bottom. Empty cells stood on either side of them. *The dungeon*, she realized. The place sent cold shivers of dread up Pearl's spine. Still, she forced her feet to keep moving. At the very end of the row of cells Faye stopped.

Pearl joined her and slowly peered in. Kale! His skin stood out in sharp contrast to the darkness around him. He came to the front and extended a hand out through the bars, groping blindly. Nervously, Pearl took it. Faye nodded slightly and then moved away, giving them privacy.

"Pearl?" he said.

"Yes."

"It seems you've met my sister," Kale noted.

"Yes," Pearl said, at a loss for what else to say.

"Are you all right?" he questioned.

"Yes. Do you know where you are?"

He laughed sharply. "Well, Faye, hasn't had a lot to say."

Pearl winced at that. "Sorry."

"Don't trouble yourself over it."

"You're in a dungeon. They say you've attacked women."

He shook his head. "That's not true. I hope you don't believe that."

She shook her head, frustrated. "I don't know what to believe, to be honest."

"Believe that I love you."

A lump rose in her throat, and she couldn't speak for a moment. Her world seemed upside down.

"Pearl, are you all right?"

"No," she sobbed. "Everything is all wrong. A week ago I had a simple life, just my parents, a close friend I might have loved, and me. Now there is just too much."

"What's too much?" he asked.

"You and Robert."

"Who is Robert?"

"Robert is a marquis, and . . . and my intended husband. I only met him the day I met you, and yet we are to marry tomorrow morning."

"No!" he shouted, throwing his whole body against the bars. "You cannot!"

Frightened, she jumped away, dropping his hand. "There is nothing I can do," she protested.

"There is everything you can do. You are a princess. It is within your power to change this. You alone have the right to say who you will marry."

His expression was fierce, and it frightened her. She took another step backward. "A princess? How can that be?"

"You are! You must see that, you must remember!"

"I must do nothing more than what I am told,"

she stammered. She backed into a cell door and barely muffled a scream as the cold metal dug into her flesh. "I—I must go," she cried, turning and fleeing back toward the stairs.

"You need to remember who you are, Adriana!" he shouted after her. "Return to the ocean and you will find yourself!"

She tripped on the stairs, falling to her knees with a painful thud. She huddled for a moment, crying in pain, before struggling back to her feet. She was relieved that Faye seemed to have disappeared.

With Kale's words echoing in her mind, she fled the castle. Startled servants marked her passage but did not try to stop her. Once free of the castle walls, she headed for the ocean.

Who am I? What did Kale mean that I was a princess and that the ocean would help me find myself? Where do I come from? A thousand questions collided in her head, crashing like the waves upon the shore.

She slowed only when she reached the sand. The blood was roaring in her ears to match the pounding of the surf. She stopped at the water's edge and stared out at the blue-green of the water. "Who am I?" she asked the seas.

The ocean was silent.

"Who am I?" she asked herself. She had been asking the question all of her life, but she had always been too afraid to hear the answer. Now she needed to know, no matter what the answer.

"I'm not human," she whispered to herself. It was

more than her physical appearance; there had always been something deep inside her that told her she didn't belong. Mary and Finneas knew, too; they had just never been able to admit it to her.

"If not human, then what?" she asked softly.

She had always felt pity for the fish that Finneas caught, though she had never had any such pity for the beasts of the land that men also ate. He had pulled her from the ocean during a storm. Kale had been in the water when the boat that she and James were in had sunk. She had found Kale sitting here beside the ocean. And something, or someone, had tried very hard to make sure that she would never step foot in the water.

It could not all be coincidence; it could all only mean one thing: She had come from the ocean. Therefore, to the ocean she would need to return to discover the truth. Maybe all those years spent sitting and staring at the ocean she had actually been searching for answers. They weren't to be found on the shore, though, she knew that now.

She picked up her skirts in one hand. Nervously grasping the pearl around her neck, she stepped into the water, taking several quick steps until she was standing in it knee-deep. "I want to know who I really am. I want to be who I really am!" she shouted.

Her legs gave way beneath her, and she crashed down into the water. She watched in stunned horror as her legs began to grow together and scales began to cover them. Pain and fear ripped through her and she scrambled backward, finally throwing herself up onto the sand. "I take it back!" she screamed. "I want to be a human!"

The pain ceased, and she lay still for a moment, too frightened to look down. At last she struggled to a sitting position. Her two legs were back as they had been: pale, gangly, and covered in human skin.

She sobbed to herself. She knew who she was. Years of searching and questioning were over. After all that seeking, she finally had the answer, but she lacked the strength to act upon it. *I am too much a coward to actually be that which I know I am,* she realized sadly.

The sun was beginning to set when she made her way, limping, back to the castle. The whole place seemed to be in an uproar, with servants and guards running about frantically. Something was wrong.

Martha was hurrying by, and Pearl caught her arm. The servant spun, startled, then hastily curtsied.

"What has happened here?"

"Someone has tried to poison the king."

"What! Who?"

"A man who was a prisoner in the dungeon. Someone helped him escape."

Pearl's blood ran cold. Kale had been the only prisoner in the dungeon. Faye must have been the one to help him escape. "Does the king live?"

"Only by the grace of God."

Pearl released Martha's arm, and the other woman rushed on her way.

"Pearl!"

She jumped at the sound of her voice and whirled toward the speaker.

It was James. His face was as dark as a thundercloud. "Come with me," he ordered, barely slowing as he passed her. Frightened, she turned to hurry behind him. Thoughts tumbled together in her head. Maybe he had heard about her dealings with Kale and Faye. Maybe he thought that she had had some part in the attempt on his father's life.

She tried to calm herself. It was useless to conjecture; it would only serve to frighten her and nothing else. She just kept moving, stumbling along behind on legs that felt even more alien to her than they had just hours before. At last they stopped, and Pearl gasped when she saw where they were.

They were in the throne room. Pearl had never been there before, but it was impossible to mistake. At one end of the room on a raised dais were two magnificent chairs the likes of which she had never seen. Guards and servants stood at every door.

"Everyone out and shut the doors!" James thundered.

Everyone hastened to comply and when the last door slammed closed, Pearl and James were all alone. Finally he stood for a moment, every inch of his frame quivering.

At last he turned to her. "You have heard what has happened."

It was a statement, not a question.

"Yes," she answered, her mouth dry.

He stood staring at her for a long minute, and she grew increasingly nervous. She finally realized, though, that he was staring *through* her rather than *at* her.

Slowly he stopped shaking, and it was as though she could physically see the fight leaving his body. He collapsed in the middle of the floor and buried his head in his hands.

She sank down next to him, unsure how to help. Hesitantly, she reached out and placed a hand on his shoulder. He tensed for a moment, and then slumped again. His body began to shudder, and she sat quietly with him, waiting for him to speak first.

At last he lifted his head and looked at her. "My father almost died today."

"I know," she whispered.

"I should have seen this coming. I've been so blind, though, so befuddled, I haven't been paying attention to the things I should have been paying attention to." He looked at her and smiled grimly. "Or the people, either."

She felt tears welling in her eyes. "Everyone understands," she whispered.

"I don't care about everyone. I care about you. I've let you down, I know that."

"No, you haven't," she denied.

"Don't lie to me, Pearl," he said, taking her hand. "No lies between us, remember?"

She nodded, not trusting her voice to speak.

"I have been a terrible judge of character, lately. I haven't been myself since that day I hit my head on the boat."

"You've just been preoccupied."

"And the more shame on me for it," he said, wincing.

She waited for him to continue. He sat quietly for a moment, but she could see from the flashing of his eyes and the twitching of his jaw that there was a storm raging inside.

"A few days ago the guards captured a criminal, a murderer. He had done things—terrible things that you shouldn't have to hear about. He has been down in the dungeon. This afternoon he escaped. He tried to poison my father. He got away. The guards are searching for him as we speak."

She began to shake uncontrollably. "Are you certain this man did the things he has been accused of?"

He nodded grimly. "And now, this. There's more. . . ." He hesitated.

Dread filled her. "What is it, James? I beg you, tell me."

He looked at her, and his eyes were filled with tenderness. "He wounded Sir Robert before he escaped. Don't fear, though, he will be all right. He's a good man and I have judged him unfairly." James snorted. "He's my better in many ways. He had the good sense to see at a glance what it took me years to figure out."

She stared deeply into his eyes and felt herself begin to tremble inside. What was the glimmer in his eye? For a wild moment she thought he was going to kiss her. "What about Faye?" she whispered.

"Faye." His voice took on the hard edge again. "Well, it seems that Faye is the one who helped him escape. It turns out that she is his sister. I was a fool."

"Maybe you're judging her too harshly. Maybe her brother was falsely accused," Pearl protested.

"No hope of that, I'm afraid. A witness has come forth who positively identified him yesterday."

Pearl felt as though the world were crashing around her. Kale was a murderer and Faye his accomplice. Had they been trying to use her in some way in their plan to kill the king? She felt as though she was going to be sick.

"Pearl, I don't want you to worry yourself about any of this now," James told her, again speaking in a gentle voice.

"Why?" she questioned through her tears.

"You have more important things to be worrying about right now."

He stood up abruptly and held out his hands to her. She clasped them, and he helped her to her feet. He held her hands for a moment and stared down at them. He ran his thumbs lightly over the backs of them before lifting his eyes to stare into hers.

"Pearl, I really do wish you and Robert the best of

luck. I know you'll be very happy together. Don't worry about the things I've told you. I just want you to relax and enjoy your wedding day tomorrow."

Solemnly, he leaned forward and kissed her on the cheek. Then he released her hands and turned on his heel, striding quickly from the room. As the door slammed shut behind him, she fell to her knees and sobbed.

❖ Chapter Eleven ❖

It was deathly silent, so when the doors of the chapel were flung open, everyone jumped. Pearl's eyes flew open as a voice rang out.

"I object!"

Pearl spun around as everyone gasped.

There at the far end of the aisle stood Kale. He was covered in dirt and blood, and his hair was matted down. His clothes hung in tatters from his body.

From the front row, James leaped to his feet. "Seize him!" he ordered.

Kale sprinted up the aisle toward her, and Pearl took a step backward. He nearly reached her before three guards tackled him to the ground. He strained his head upward, his sightless eyes staring past her.

"Don't! Pearl, don't throw your life away on someone you don't love!"

"Why did you come here?" she shouted above the hubbub.

"Because I love you," he cried.

"But by coming here you've killed yourself," she cried, dropping to her knees before him.

"Without your love, I am dead at sunset, anyway," he whispered, for her ears alone.

The guards hauled him to his feet and dragged him back toward the entrance.

Pearl stood back up. "What do you mean by that?" she called.

He didn't answer, or if he did, she could not hear.

"Wait!" she cried, racing after him. "What do you mean by that?"

"Ask the Sea Witch!" Just then, one of the guards hit him, knocking him unconscious. His body slumped between them, and they carried him the rest of the way out of the church, closing the doors behind them.

Slowly, the guests reclaimed their seats. Mary and Finneas remained standing, though, hovering close to Pearl.

"Carry on, good priest, 'twas just the ramblings of a madman," James instructed, reclaiming his seat.

Robert took her hand and tried to pull her back. She resisted, still staring at the closed doors. The Sea Witch, Kale had said. The words struck a chord somewhere in her being. *Where have I heard that name?* she asked herself.

"Milady, with your permission, we will continue," Father Gregory told her.

She turned to stare at him, and he just stared back. She remembered her first Sunday service, sitting and listening to the old priest and only understanding every other word. He had intimidated her a little bit with his grim complexion. He had reminded her of her father as he lectured her about watching out for the Sea Witch.

Her father. An image filled her mind, and the face didn't belong to Finneas. She saw a long, thin nose and a broad brow topped with a wreath of seaweed laced through with large, white pearls. She had always wanted the pearls. He had told her when she was old enough she would have some of her own because she was a princess. *Princess! Kale had been right! He and Faye were mer-kin too!*

She turned to look at Robert while she spoke to Father Gregory. "I'm sorry, I can't. I just can't."

Robert's eyes widened in shock. She bent forward and kissed his cheek. "I'm sorry, but I can't accept your kind offer. I belong someplace else, and I have to find out exactly where that is."

She pulled her hand from his and fled down the aisle amidst shouts of consternation.

"Pearl!" she heard Robert shouting. "Come back!"

James sat, stunned, as Pearl raced from the church. Sir Robert, his leg slightly wounded from his brush with the criminal yesterday, stood looking thunderstruck. A wave of pity washed over James, mixed with an overwhelming sensation of relief.

His thoughts flew back to Pearl as he caught Mary staring at him in bewilderment. *What has gotten into Pearl?* He wasn't sure what it was, but he knew it had something to do with what the criminal had said to her. Just then, a footman slipped up to him and bent to whisper in his ear. "The king is awake and he is asking for you."

He rose quickly to his feet and exited through a side door.

Within minutes he was in his father's bedchamber.

His father was sitting, fully clothed, in a chair next to the window, with Peter standing beside him. He chuckled as James came in. "Well, how did it feel to almost be king?"

"Terrible," James replied, not amused. "Shouldn't you be in bed?"

The king waved his hand. "I'm fine, James. The poison clarrey never touched my lips."

"What!" James exploded.

"No—however, I wanted others to think that it had."

"Why didn't you tell me?"

King Philip sighed. "I needed your reactions to be realistic if my plan is to work."

"What plan?" James asked, in a moment moving from angry to bewildered.

"My plan to catch the duke and his son at their own game."

"But, I thought that the criminal—"

The king snorted. "That poor fellow is no criminal . . . at least not to my knowledge. Robert made

171

him out to be one only to further his own schemes. He and his father were planning on killing me and blaming it on an escaped criminal."

"So, they released him."

"Actually, I released him," Peter spoke up.

"But why?" James asked.

"To force their hand," the king answered.

"It looks like it worked."

"Only partially," Peter answered. "We don't have actual proof that it was either of them who poisoned the drink."

"So, your plan failed," James asserted.

"No, it did not. The poisoner did leave this behind." Peter held up an elaborate man's ring with a large onyx stone. The top swung open to reveal a tiny hollow just large enough to hold a bit of poison powder. "This shouldn't be too hard to trace."

"How did you know about the poison?"

"Your father hasn't eaten or drank anything that hasn't first been tested for months."

"So, some poor servant is dead?"

"On the contrary, it's a mouse that is dead," Peter said with a laugh. "Poor little fellow keeled right over."

James felt himself sag with relief, then he rubbed his head. "I can't believe you two didn't tell me about all this."

"I could say the same about you and your little friend Pearl. She certainly did not escape the duke's notice. It was unfortunate, indeed, that she has, shall we say, distinctive characteristics that are shared by the man who was imprisoned."

"Robert was marrying Pearl as part of the plot against you and you knew about it!" James exploded. "Why didn't you stop it?"

"It was better to have her linked to him than to you. Had you married her, the duke could have implicated you in my death. Of course, with the arrival of Faye, he could have done that, anyway. Especially since she actually seems to be the accused man's sister."

"We think that originally they intended to blackmail you regarding your relationship with Pearl. Then, when they realized your intentions toward her might be more serious, Robert decided to propose to her to throw you off balance. All along they planned to imprison a man, innocent or criminal, have him escape and murder you and me. When Faye and the other man showed up, it accelerated their plans greatly. Suddenly they could say that the two did it together and you were plotting with them because of your obvious affection for Faye and your suggesting that Robert marry Pearl."

"But I never suggested that Robert marry Pearl!" James protested.

"Didn't you?" the king asked. "You were the one who told him to propose to a commoner. You were the one eager to find for your little friend an alternative to the blacksmith. That's the story he told to everyone but you."

James shook his head, marveling at how close

they had come to complete disaster. *And all because I was too distracted to realize that something was terribly wrong.* He turned his anger on his father. "How can you participate in all these machinations, these deceptions?"

"Dear boy, I did not get to be king by chance. I have worked long and hard to keep this throne and I will pass it on to you. When you are in my position you will understand these things. You will also learn to be more discrete in your friendships."

"Discrete? Discrete? You're a fine one to talk about that, Father. You and Peter have been best friends for how many years? I don't think anyone is fooled by the servant act, least of all me."

"We've never hidden our friendship from you, James. Peter and I grew up together, without worry of social boundaries, as you and your friend have done. For years he has been a loyal friend and a wise counselor. He keeps me informed of all the goings-on around here, including the schemes of the duke and his son.

"If it weren't for Peter, I wouldn't have given you nearly as much freedom. Do you truly think that you managed to elude all the tutors and all the castle guard every single week? No, Peter told them all to turn a blind eye. He has always been an advocate for you. Even with this marriage business he has been urging me to give you time to work things out for yourself."

King Philip snorted. "Though at the rate you work

things out for yourself, I'll be many years in my grave before I have a grandson. They're both fine girls. Just pick one of them and marry her, son. Get on with it."

James was speechless. All this time he had never fooled his father, only himself.

The king shook his head wearily. "I'm sorry, son. I should have trusted you and told you what we were up to. I promise you can help us smoke out the culprit from here on out," he said, taking the ring from Peter and holding it up for inspection.

"Allow me to save you the trouble," a voice said from the door.

Surprised, James turned to see the duke Stephen standing there, a sword in hand. "My son tends to be overly subtle. He likes complicated plans. Personally, I've found that the direct approaches work best."

"What do you plan on doing?" James demanded, moving in front of his father.

"Simple, I will kill the three of you."

"And who will you blame it on? Your 'murderer' is back in custody."

"Not anymore," the duke sneered. "It seems he managed to escape the guardsmen, killing all of them. Of course, he has me to thank for that. Then he came here to finish what he started. Never fear, though. I shall catch him along with his sister and friend, and they shall all three hang for your murders. It will then be with a heavy heart that I ascend the throne as the closest blood relative."

"You're mad," James told him.

"Who will stop me?"

James cursed the lack of weapon within reach of any of them. He started to circle the duke, calculating how best to attack and attempt to disarm him. He knew the duke was a wicked fighter, much like his son.

Before he could make his move, though, Peter lunged. The duke whirled, slashing Peter across the stomach and sending him crashing to the ground. He raised his sword, preparing to deliver a killing blow.

A vase smashed into the duke's back. The duke staggered, stunned, and James lunged toward him. The king beat him there, though. From his boot, the king pulled a small dagger and plunged it into the duke's heart before the other could swing at him. The duke collapsed on the ground beside Peter. His eyes rolled backward before they fixed in his head, and his body slumped.

James turned toward the door and saw Faye standing there, shaking. "Thank you, my dear, you saved us all," the king boomed from behind him.

Servants dashed past her and moved over to Peter. "I'm going to be fine," he protested as they set to work tending his wound.

James turned and strode to Faye. He pulled her out into the hallway and held her hands in his. He looked deep into her eyes. "This is twice now that you have saved me. I'm going to have to keep you around," he said with a smile.

His smile faded. "Faye, I love you. I have loved you since the first moment that I saw you. Something in my blood cries out to you, and I know that I want to be with you. Will you marry me?"

She nodded, tears streaming down her cheeks. He kissed her.

Faye felt that her heart would burst with happiness. James loved her and was going to marry her! She had won and now she could remain human and stay with him. She would live and love. Her only regret was that he would never be able to hear her say how much she loved him. The Sea Witch might have lost the gamble, but she still kept her fee.

James pulled away from her to go check on the injured man. Her thoughts turned to Kale. She didn't know where he was, but she hoped Pearl was with him. She was safe, but her brother's time was running out.

Behind the church, Pearl found the bodies of the soldiers who had dragged Kale from the chapel. Kale lay to the side. He groaned slightly and sat up, rubbing at his head.

She dropped down next to him and touched his face.

He stiffened. "Who is it?"

"Someone you love," she whispered.

"Pearl! What happened?"

"I don't know, but this does not look good. Can you walk?"

He nodded. She helped him stand and led him quickly from the scene, heading for the ocean where they would be safe from prying eyes.

"Did you marry him?"

"No, I didn't love him."

A look of relief flooded his face.

When they had put some distance between them and the church, she asked him the one question she needed answered. "Tell me about the Sea Witch."

"Do you remember anything?"

"Not really. All I know is that I—I'm a . . . mermaid." It was both odd and something of a relief to say it aloud.

He stopped short and turned to her. "Well, that is a start."

"Yes," she laughed. "Now, the Witch?"

"She was banished years ago by our people. She lives in a cave. She's trapped there, unable to leave. A strand of pearls around her neck is the source of her power."

She fingered the pearl around her own neck. Could it have some connection with the Witch's pearls?

"Although her caves are forbidden, from time to time a mermaid or merman seeks her out for magical help."

"To become human?" Pearl guessed.

He nodded. "But her help always comes with a price. For me, it was my sight. For Faye, her voice."

"You both must have wanted very much to be human."

"Yes. Faye paid an even higher price than that."

"How so?"

"If the prince agrees to marry her, by sunset on the seventh day she will remain human forever."

"And if she doesn't?"

"She will die."

Chills danced up Pearl's spine. "Then that means . . ."

"She only has a little time left."

"Come on," Pearl cried, grabbing his hand.

"Where are we going?"

"To save Faye."

Faye hurried toward the church. Her heart was filled to overflowing with love for James. He had asked her to marry him! She would be human now forever, and they would spend their lives together. She had bet the Sea Witch and had won.

Her thoughts turned toward her brother. Kale, on the other hand, only had a short while left before he would die. She had to find a way to bring him and Pearl together.

She circled around the church and nearly tripped over the body of a dead guardsman. Stunned, she stared. He had been one of the men who had dragged Kale from the church. Where was her brother, though?

"Looking for someone?" a voice hissed in her ear.

She jumped, but Robert grabbed her around the waist and pressed a dagger against her ribs. "You're my revenge. I can hurt the prince through you. You're coming with me."

If she had had her voice, she would have screamed, but without it, she had no choice but to go along.

❖ Chapter Twelve ❖

There was only about half an hour left until sunset. Pearl stood inches from the water. She took a deep breath, trying to calm herself.

"I love you, Pearl," Kale whispered.

"I love you, too."

She looked at him. He looked so vulnerable as he stood there in the light of the waning sun. She kissed him and he kissed her back, sending shivers down her body. She pulled back and looked at him, brushing a lock of hair out of his face.

He had said that the prince must agree to marry Faye by sunset or she would die. He hadn't told her what bargain he had made with the Sea Witch, but she guessed it was something similar.

"When this is all over, Kale, I will marry you," she promised him.

A mingled look of joy and despair crossed his face, and he kissed her again. She was puzzled at his expression, but did not have time to question him about it.

"I wish I could go with you."

"I know, but this is something I have to do by myself."

He nodded. "Just remember, the pearls are the key to the Witch's power. Without them, she is nothing."

She moved away from him and took a step toward the ocean. She stood at the water's edge, with fear wrapping around her heart. She clasped the pearl in her hand. The water lapped at her toes. *I was playing with Kale by a sunken boat,* she recalled. She took a step into the water. *He was my best friend.* She took another step, the water lapping against both her ankles. *It was almost dinnertime, and I left to go home.* Another step and the waves lapped at her calves. *A shadow darkened the water, and I turned to see what it was.* The water was swirling around her knees.

The Sea Witch was there, more terrible than Father had said she was. Her skirts slogged around her legs as the water crept up her legs. *She grabbed me and I couldn't fight her, she was too strong. She clamped her hand over my mouth so I could not scream.* The water was at her waist and growing deeper. *She took me back to her cave.* The water was chest-deep and warm, so very warm. *She cursed me. She turned me into a human.* She looked down, and her legs were disappearing, merging into a shimmering tail covered with scales. *She told me I was nobody, nothing. She wasn't interested in me, she just wanted to hurt my family.* Her hair was floating on top of the water and it began to glow. *She sent me to the surface to either drown or live upon the land. I snatched this pearl from her necklace before the seas tossed me upward.* Her clothes fell from her, the beautiful blue wedding dress drifting away with the current. . . . *She said that if I returned to the ocean I would die.* She took in her mermaid body, noticing the way her skin shone under the water. *She was wrong about that. She said I was nothing, that I could not harm her.* She clutched the pearl around her neck. *The Witch was wrong about that, too.*

With a flick of her tail, she dove beneath the surface. She breathed the water as naturally as though she had never forgotten how. She was the princess, Adriana, child of the mer-kin.

She remembered.

She remembered everything, including where to find the Witch.

Kale heard the splash as she dove beneath the surface of the water. It had worked. She had broken the spell binding her. He sank to a seat on the beach, overcome with emotion. She had agreed to marry him. In that one moment she had both saved him and doomed him. She had saved his life while yet cursing him to live out his days as a human. Now that she was once again a mermaid, they were again of two separate worlds. He had lost her a second time.

He sat and waited, counting out the minutes in his head and feeling the retreating rays of the sun upon his skin. The minutes of Faye's life were slipping away, and there was nothing he could do to stop it. Just as he judged that time was nearly up, pain ripped through him. He screamed and fell backward, writhing on the sand.

Pearl dove farther down into the darkness, the light from her hair all she needed to see her way. Her people had defeated the Sea Witch, Kale had said, but they had been unable to kill her. They had locked her instead in a set of underwater caves from which she should not have been able to escape.

She had, though. She had harnessed the magic from an ancient strand of midnight pearls to enable her to come and go as she pleased. She had left the cave and kidnapped Pearl. Her father had warned her never to go near the caves where the Witch lived, not dreaming that it would make no difference where she was.

She swam swiftly, her tail working better than her legs ever had. She thought about Faye when she had led her through the castle to see Kale. Within a couple of days the young woman was moving with more grace on land than Pearl had managed to achieve in thirteen years. She shook her head, astounded.

The water rushed by her skin, cool and comforting, welcoming her home. She wondered if her parents had ever had another child; she had been their firstborn. She remembered her mother's gentle touch, her father's strong embrace. She longed to see them again, to be with them. First, though, she had business with the Sea Witch.

A dolphin came close to her, whistling a greeting.

He approached so close that she was able to reach out and touch him. She thrilled at the contact, and at the memory of riding upon one as a child. Mer-kin could communicate with the creatures of the sea, she remembered. Together, they spiraled downward until he finally broke off to return to the surface. She continued onward.

At last she was close to the Witch's lair. She could feel it in the water around her, in the way the cold suddenly began to seep into her bones. Her heart trembled for a moment, but she pressed on. She was no longer a child, helpless to defend herself against the Witch. She was a woman, and she, too, had magic.

At the entrance to the caves she stopped and hovered in the water, tail flipping slowly back and forth.

"Come in," a voice called out to her. It washed over her, slippery as a serpent.

"Why don't you come out?" Pearl taunted.

There was silence for a moment, and then the Witch appeared just inside the entrance to the cave. "Come in, my child, and I can help you with whatever you desire."

"Can't you come out to me?" Pearl asked, all innocence. "I'm afraid of the dark."

"Unfortunately, my dear, I cannot leave these caves. They are my home."

"I can leave my home, why can't you leave yours?"

"I was cursed, child, cursed to live my life in these caves never to step outside."

"I thought I saw you outside the cave before."

"You must be mistaken. Now come inside and we can discuss you and what you came here to ask for," the Witch said, sounding irritated.

"So, you are unable to ever leave?"

The Witch stroked her pearls. "Apparently. Now, what is it you are here for? Are you looking for love, fame, or perhaps are you searching for something you have lost?"

"Actually, I'm here to discuss something you have lost," Pearl said. She held out the necklace with the pearl on it.

"Give that to me!" the Witch shrieked, flinging herself forward. The pearls around her neck were glowing bright. At the very lip of the cave she slammed into some sort of invisible wall and was thrown backward.

"So, without the entire set of pearls, you really are powerless to leave here," Pearl noted as the Witch gathered herself up, glowering.

"The only way you can harm mer-kin is to get them to come inside to you. Without this one tiny pearl, you can no longer come out to them." She slipped the necklace back on. "It's ironic, don't you think, that in kidnapping me, you doomed yourself? I was able to live a full life on the land, while you were trapped here in your caves. I guess you could say that you lost more than I did, especially since I had no memory of the life I left behind."

Power surged through Pearl, and she drifted to

within a half inch of the barrier, daring the Witch to try to snatch the pearl from around her neck. The foul creature tried, flinging herself again against the barrier only to be repulsed once more.

"I had thought of killing you," Pearl answered. "But death would be far too kind for you. Instead, I'm going to let you live out your days here, alone. And mark my words, I shall see to it that no mer-kin ever enters your lair again."

"Who are you?" the Witch whispered, her face contorted in a snarl.

She laughed and floated backward in the water. "I am Adriana, princess of the mer-kin, kidnapped by you and sent to live among humans." She smiled slyly. "But you can call me Pearl."

She stroked the pearl around her neck, and a low rumble filled the water. "I renounce your magic. I restore those whom you have cursed. And you, you are nothing more than a bad dream."

A slab of rock from higher up on the mountain slid down and covered the entrance to the caves, sealing the Witch in and keeping all others out. As the stone settled into place, even the scream of the Sea Witch was lost, sealed in for eternity.

Pearl turned and shot back toward the surface, swimming as fast as she could. The magic binding the Witch to the caves had been strong, and only the strength of all the pearls together could break it. Each individual pearl was powerful, but it needed all of them to overcome the other magic that had been used to banish the Witch. Without the one pearl that she had taken from the Witch, the Witch had been unable to overcome the magic binding her to the cave. There was a lot of power in that one little pearl, enough to allow Pearl to do what she needed.

His vision returned in a sudden, crippling blow. He saw the last ray of the setting sun disappear beneath the horizon. What was happening? He tried to sit up but could not. He glanced downward and saw his legs growing back into a tail. He began to gasp, the air searing his lungs. He flipped over on his stomach and dug his hands into the sand, propelling himself toward the water.

When the pain stopped and his head cleared, he realized that Pearl had done it. She had defeated the Sea Witch and in the process had reversed all of her spells. He turned to search the waves for Pearl, eager to see her. Suddenly, fear knifed through him. Faye! Faye would be transformed back into a mermaid, too, and she was still in the middle of the village.

Faye screamed as the transformation began. She recognized it for what it was and wailed in anguish. *Not now!* James had asked her to marry him. She couldn't go back.

Robert clutched her tighter. "Stop struggling," he hissed in her ear.

She couldn't help it. As the pain overtook her, she

writhed in agony. He cursed at her, but she was beyond caring about him and his schemes. *No!* her mind screamed even as her body changed. Fear ripped through her as she began to gasp for breath.

Robert screamed as her scales rose up from her back and pierced his body. Then he collapsed onto the ground and she fell atop him. He gasped once, and then lay still. She knew that he was dead.

Villagers came running and when they saw her tail and the dead marquis, they began to shout. Many hands grabbed at her, and she didn't have the strength to fight them off.

"Witch!" someone yelled, and others took up the shout. Her head swam as she continued to gasp for breath. Suddenly she was lifted into the air. They placed her against a post and lashed her to it, the ropes cutting into her skin until her blood flowed freely.

She stared blankly from face to face; they all began to blur in her vision. At last her sight faded, and everything went black.

Mary was worried. She and Finneas had left the church in search of Pearl but had been unable to find her. They couldn't even find Faye or the prince. Frustrated, they began walking through the village, looking for familiar faces.

"Do you think she would have gone to the ocean?"

"It seems to me that's where she goes whenever she's upset," Finneas answered.

Together, they turned and began walking toward the water. Mary just hoped Pearl was all right. She sighed. The last few days had not been easy on anyone, but who could have anticipated all this?

Suddenly, she stopped, listening. "Do you hear that?" she asked.

Finneas stopped and listened too. "Sounds like someone shouting."

"Sounds like several people."

Then one word rang clear through the air. Someone cried, "Witch!"

Mary turned and began to run back the way they had come. Her blood turned to ice water in her veins. It was a word she had long prayed not to hear, and on today, of all days, it was not a good omen.

Shouts of anger spurred Mary on to run even faster. When they reached the square, her heart flew into her throat. There was a girl lashed to a wooden beam. Flames were licking at her feet. The fire reflected off her silver hair. *Pearl!*

"No!" Mary screamed as she raced forward. Beside her she heard Finneas shouting.

She picked up a bucket of water standing nearby and doused the flames as Finneas shouted at the angry crowd.

She glanced up at the face of the girl and felt herself sag in relief. It was Faye. Something was wrong with her, though, she was too still. It was then that Mary saw the tail where the girl's legs had once been. She gasped aloud. *A mermaid!* Suddenly everything made sense. Tears swam in her eyes. This, then, was what her Pearl was as well.

Faye was so still, Mary thought she might already be dead. She couldn't let herself think that way, though. If the girl was a mermaid, then she was like a fish. Fish didn't do well outside of water, but some could certainly live longer than others.

She picked up another bucket of water and doused her with it, aiming at her face and torso. Faye gasped, and her chest heaved as the water entered her mouth.

Villagers jumped back with shouts of "Witchcraft" on their lips.

Finneas's voice boomed out. "Aye, 'tis witchcraft, but not of this young one's doing. She has been cursed by an evil Witch."

Good thinking, Finneas, Mary thought.

The crowd quieted slightly, listening to what he had to say. "It is part of a plot to kill our beloved king. The king lives, though, and this girl helped save him. That's why the Witch has tried to kill her."

He pointed to the body of the fallen marquis. "Behold, the marquis was another victim of her evil."

There were murmurs of anxiety as everyone began crossing themselves. Suddenly there was a shout, and the crowd parted as though by magic.

Prince James strode up to them. "What is happening here?" he boomed.

He saw Faye, and his face turned ash white. For a moment Mary was afraid he would faint. He regained his composure, though, and turned to the crowd. "It is true, what this man says. An evil Witch has attacked the kingdom. We have, all of us, been saved, though, by this girl and by Pearl."

Ragged cheering rose as Mary helped James cut the ropes binding Faye to the post. She slumped into his arms, and Mary splashed more water on her face.

"You must get her to the sea, and quickly, Your Highness," she advised him.

He looked at her with tears streaming down his face. "Yes, of course, you are right."

He picked her up and called for a horse. One was at his side in a moment, and he mounted with Faye in his arms. He kicked the beast into action, and Mary and Finneas ran in its wake.

"How did you know the king was all right?" Mary gasped as they ran.

"I didn't, I was bluffing," Finneas admitted.

They arrived at the ocean shortly after James did. The prince was crouching in the water, holding Faye and splashing water over her face. As they watched, the girl began to move and finally she looked up at him. He bent down and kissed her once. She then slipped from his arms and into the sea.

Mary rushed forward but hesitated when she reached the prince. He looked up at her. "Pearl too?" he asked.

"I think so," she whispered as she crouched beside him. They knelt together in the water, mourning.

❖❖❖❖

Pearl broke the surface of the water near the beach. She scanned it for a sign of Kale, but there was none. That was a good sign that what she had done had worked. She flipped her tail up and slapped it on the surface of the water.

Moments later, Kale's head popped up. Delighted, she ducked back beneath the water and swam to him. He met her halfway and caught her in his arms. Their tails wrapped around each other as they kissed.

At last they broke apart. "Faye?" Pearl said.

A cloud passed across his face. "I don't think she made it," he said. "When you broke all the spells the Sea Witch had cast, it turned me back into a merman. I barely made it into the water. Faye was still in the village. I don't know how she could have made it."

"I am so sorry, Kale," Pearl sobbed, wrapping her arms around him.

"It's not your fault. There was nothing we could do," he told her.

They drifted closer to the shore, holding each other, comforting each other. Slowly, a new sound intruded upon Pearl's subconscious. It was a splashing sound. She lifted her head out of the water and stared toward the shore.

She saw Mary and Finneas on the shore. James was in the water and he was holding something. *Faye!*

Quickly, she and Kale headed for them. Before they made it there, a new sound emerged in the water, and suddenly Faye collided with them. She was wide-eyed with despair and threw herself into Kale's arms. He held her close, trying to soothe her, and Pearl lifted her head out of the water again. She saw Mary and James huddled together in the water and she could feel their pain.

She ducked back down and looked at Faye. "Faye, do you love him?" she asked.

"Yes," the girl cried, turning to look at her.

"Do you love him enough to live out there with him?"

"Of course. He had asked me to marry him and I would have stayed with him, gladly."

"Come with me, then," Pearl said, grabbing the other mermaid's hand.

They swam toward the shore, Kale following them. When they were close to Mary and James, they stopped and broke the surface. "James," Pearl called.

He looked up, startled. The joy that flooded his face made her heart sing. He had always been her dearest friend. He had given her so much, and now there was something that she could give him. The other two hung back as she moved toward James.

"How long have you known?" he asked wonderingly.

"Only a day," she told him. "I was kidnapped as a child and turned into a human by the Sea Witch."

He laughed through his tears. "I always told you there was magic in the world."

"And you were right," she told him. "Do you love Faye?"

"Heaven help me, I do," he told her.

"Would you marry her if she could live in your world?"

"Tonight, if she would have me."

Pearl turned to Mary and Finneas, who had come up beside her. "Would you both watch after Faye as though she were your own daughter?"

"As though she were you," Mary said, touching her face.

Pearl nodded and then turned. "Faye," she called.

The other mermaid floated up, fear and hope mixing in her eyes. Pearl took the necklace from her neck and placed it around Faye's. "The pearl is magic, and I want you to keep it safe for me. It will help you be who you truly are. You just need to look in your own heart."

Faye closed her eyes. "I want to be that which I truly am inside," she said, clutching the pearl.

Before her eyes, Faye's tail split once more into legs, and her skin lost its scales. Slowly she stood in the water and James stood with her, wrapping his arms around her and kissing her.

Mary smiled up at them before turning back to Pearl. "I'm going to miss you, daughter."

"And I, you, Mama," Pearl told her, embracing her.

Mary nodded at Kale. "Make sure he takes good care of you."

"I will, Mama."

"And make sure you come to visit from time to time," Finneas added gruffly.

"Papa, look out for your nets," Pearl laughed as she hugged him.

They parted, and Kale swam forward, taking her hand. Together they turned and dove into the ocean.

Pearl was sad to leave the others behind, but her heart lifted the deeper they went. *I can always go back and visit,* she told herself.

"Do you still want to marry me?" Kale asked as they swam.

She turned to him. "More than ever."

A smile broke across his face, and they dove together, racing around each other.

After a while she could see a tiny pinprick of light ahead in the darkness. It grew brighter as they drew near. *Home,* she realized with a thrill.

"Are you nervous?" Kale asked.

She nodded. "A little bit."

He grinned as he grabbed her hand. "Don't worry. You defeated the Sea Witch today. This will be easy."

She smiled into his eyes and held his gaze as they sailed into the sphere of light. They stopped, and she looked around cautiously. Dozens of mer-kin surrounded them, with dozens more arriving by the second. An older merman came to the front. "Son!"

"Father!" Kale cried, embracing the other.

"Where's your sister?"

"It's a long story, Dad, but she's safe and sound.

Right now, I'd like to introduce you to someone. Her name is Pearl, but we all knew her as Adriana."

"Adriana?" he gasped.

Kale nodded as the cry was taken up by the rest. Kale squeezed her hand, giving her strength. Suddenly the cry died down and a path cleared. An older couple swam toward them. They each wore a crown of seaweed strewn with white pearls.

"Mother, Father!" she cried, recognizing them. She let go of Kale's hand and flew into their outstretched arms. They held her close, and all three babbled incoherently.

Minutes passed before her father regained his composure and stretched out his arm to Kale. The merman joined them.

"I owe you a great debt for restoring our daughter to us."

"Your daughter has consented to marry me, that is all I need."

He beamed upon them both. "Well, then, let's get this wedding underway. I believe the two of you have waited long enough. After all, a seventeen-year engagement must be a record."

As she laughed, Pearl felt encompassed by warmth and understanding. As Kale's lips met hers, she knew that she had found the home she had been searching for.

Debbie Viguié is the coauthor of the Wicked series. Debbie has been writing since she was eight and counts it as one of the great passions of her life. She and her husband, Scott, currently live in Anaheim, California, where they indulge their mutual passion for theme parks. Her Web site is www.debbieviguie.com.

"Once upon a time . . ."

is timely once again as fresh, quirky heroines breathe life into classic and much-loved characters.

Reknowned heroines master newfound destinies, uncovering a unique and original "happily ever after. . . ."

Historical romance and magic unite in modern retellings of well-loved tales.

✦✦✦✦✦

THE STORYTELLER'S DAUGHTER
by Cameron Dokey

BEAUTY SLEEP
by Cameron Dokey

SNOW
by Tracy Lynn

MIDNIGHT PEARLS
by Debbie Viguié